On the Market

On the Market

A Texas BBQ Brothers Romance

Audrey Wick

TULE
PUBLISHING

Dedication

This book is dedicated to Barbara Collins Rosenberg.

Acknowledgements

My debut year of writing occurred with the launch of my Texas Sisters series. This year, brothers get their turn but in a new location: Tule Publishing's world of Last Stand.

Jane Porter, thank you for creating this world and inviting authors into it. Meghan Farrell, I appreciate your early reading of my manuscript and, Jenny Silver, thank you for helping build the town. Cyndi, Nicole, Dominique, Lee, and Monti, your help behind the scenes at Tule allows these stories to reach readers.

Joanne Rock, our early conversation about Last Stand and your willingness to help brainstorm placed me on the right track for this idea. Thank you for mentoring me on this project.

Beth Wiseman, you continue to be a mentor as well through your support and friendship. Here's to more lunchtime conversations, writing retreats, and story talk. And to Janet Murphy, thank you for offering a room with a view to help me work on this novel.

Julie Sturgeon, you helped me focus the lens on this by working in partnership as an editor to create a better story. You also did so with good humor and kindness all along the way.

I am grateful to pitmaster Mark Prause in La Grange, Texas, for answering my questions about the barbeque world. Readers, if you want food as delicious as what's served in The Hut, visit Prause's meat market. You won't be disappointed.

Special thanks go to *The Fayette County Record* staff and The Gallery at Round Top for selling paperback copies of my books and supporting my projects locally.

Mike and Lisa Corker, gratitude for borrowing Nod's name for the book. He's a neighborhood joy!

Brian Cravens, writing is possible because of the support and love you give.

Luke, thank you for being proud of the work I do—and for loving vegetables.

Finally, Barbara Collins Rosenberg, you believed in my writing and helped me tell this story. Thank you for your advocacy as my agent. It's my pleasure to dedicate this book to you.

Chapter One

HUTCH SQUARED OFF with Cole across a table in the dining area of their family business. Hutchinson's barbeque market may be an institution in Last Stand, Texas, but the way the brothers had been feuding lately made the restaurant's interior seem more like a wrestling ring.

Cole splayed his hands wide, stretching each finger before slackening them enough to continue hammering his latest idea. "The entrance of this place is really the problem. If we reconfigure, we'll be able to draw in more customers and create a positive first impression for everyone who walks into The Hut."

Hutch pinched the bridge of his nose, sighing heavily as he fought to stay still in his seat. "This is a barbeque market, not a sunroom."

"But we can make it more welcoming." Cole edged his crude, two-dimensional sketches across the table, as if forcing Hutch to see them up close would somehow change his mind.

Nope.

Hutch crossed his arms over his chest. "You're talking like someone on a Hollywood home renovation show."

"Maybe that's what we need around here." Cole raised his hand to gesture around the dining space that lay empty after their lunchtime rush. "This place is so stuck in the eighties that I hear Willie Nelson songs in my head every time I walk through it."

"Is that a bad thing?"

Cole blew out his breath in a slow-roasted release.

Hutch had gotten under his brother's skin. That was where he wanted to be because Cole had been singing this same tune for months and Hutch was tired of hearing it. "There's something to be said for tradition."

"We have that. It's in what we serve." Cole paused. "But it doesn't have to be in where we serve it."

Hutch wasn't sure if he was hearing Cole right. "We're staying in this location." Hutchinson's barbeque market had been on Main Street, right in the heart of the town for three generations.

"I never said we weren't. I wouldn't think of moving from here."

At least the brothers agreed on that.

"This piece of real estate is far too precious. People know us here."

And that was Hutch's reasoning for keeping things as they were. "That's right. They know us. And they expect certain things."

"Quality. Value." Cole wasn't arguing those points. "But we still have to keep this place presentable. And if we don't modernize, we aren't going to grow. People nowadays expect more than what they see in here."

Hutch didn't have a problem with what he saw. True, the style was a bit dated. But everything was kept clean and neat. Nothing cried for immediate repair. There were no holes in the wall, no leaky roof, and no cracks in the floor. Hutch uncrossed his arms, relaxing a bit. "This is our family business. And since it's coming into our hands, we have responsibilities to uphold."

"Which is why if we just reconfigure the entrance, we can save—"

"We're not reconfiguring anything." Hutch fought the urge to stand up and storm off. "The entrance is what makes this place special. It takes every customer right by the barbeque pits."

The Hut's pits were legendary. They had been built by hand by Bubba Hutchinson, the boys' grandfather, as well as their own father. As much a labor of love as market show-pieces, those pits were the epicenter of their entire business.

"Nobody cares about seeing those pits now."

"People do care." Every day, Hutch watched people light up at the site of where the magic happened. "Maybe you're just too busy being bent over those pits to see what's right in front of you."

"What's right in front of me"—Cole balled his fist and set it firmly on the tabletop between them—"is years of service smoking the meats that bring people through the doors in the first place. And all I'm trying to do is make those doors a bit grander."

Hutch shook his head. "Wasted space."

Cole continued full steam ahead. "Then once we recon-figure the entrance, we can showcase a bigger menu with more options like these." He unballed his fist to shift the papers that lay between them like an olive branch. He thumbed through the stack and procured a list that Hutch didn't recognize.

"What's that?" Hutch reached for the sheet but recoiled as if a snake bit the moment he read the words. "Vegetables?" He nearly gagged.

"These are expanded menu options," Cole corrected.

But the words Hutch read were as dirty as any in a carnivore's vocabulary. "Corn casserole, brussels sprouts, baby spinach salad, baked artichoke?" Each was more shocking than the previous. He pushed the papers back toward Cole. "What kind of operation are you trying to run here?"

"I'm trying to cater to new clientele."

"All your ideas are leaving a bad taste in my mouth." Hutch swallowed hard.

"Just think about it. Don't let a first impression sour you on what could be good for business five, ten, fifteen years down the road." Cole slid the papers again toward him.

"I *am* thinking years down the road. Fad menu options and trendy interiors come and go. Classic, traditional fare in an atmosphere that people have come to expect is what's going to matter into the future."

"I think you're overreacting to the changes." Cole removed his hand from the paperwork, placing full custody of the documents in Hutch's possession. "Take these, and let's talk about this tomorrow once you have a chance to consider. You owe me that much, considering our share in this business is fifty-fifty."

Tug-of-war talks and edged compromises might be Hutch's new life moving forward. He'd always negotiated with Cole growing up, but now with business on the line, their level of negotiation took on a whole new meaning. But compromises in the business world never resulted in a win. Each party gave up something in the process, so it was a losing proposition for both sides.

Maybe he could talk to his parents about changing ownership percentages. After all, didn't birth order account for something?

Indeed, the more he thought about it, a fifty-one forty-nine split was much more appropriate for older brother versus young brother. That arrangement would lead to far less disagreement when it came to major matters like Cole was proposing, especially if Hutch could be the one on top when it came to final decisions.

"Tomorrow morning? Meet you here at eight?"

"I've got some post oaks to cut with Brody." An eight o'clock meeting wouldn't give him enough time to finish the early morning job. "Make it nine." Hutch stood from the table and took the papers.

Cole rolled his eyes. "Fine."

He had no reason to be frustrated. An hour's difference shouldn't matter in Cole's schedule in the slightest since he'd be saucing and smoking the day's cuts of meat either way. But Hutch held smug satisfaction that at least they'd both be inconvenienced.

As he turned, he folded the papers and pressed their edges together firmly, relieving as much frustration as he could. But even as he paced away from Cole, tension hung in the air, heavy as grill pit smoke.

THE LANDSCAPING HAD been picture perfect. Boxwoods framed the exterior, heirloom roses popped with color, and butterfly bushes stretched their spiny stalks in welcome. The small yard held decades of history with plants lovingly tended.

Until today.

Valerie had heard commotion outside and glimpsed a couple of guys with power tools in the neighbor's yard. She was headed to the front door to get a better look when a crash reverberated the windowpanes and doorframes of the bungalow with earthquake force. Valerie's freshly brewed mug of coffee slipped from her fingers and collided with the tile floor. She winced as her bare legs stung with heat from the splash.

Swinging open the front door to sidestep the mess, she met the cause of the commotion head-on. She cinched her thigh-high bathrobe tightly as she prepared to confront trouble in the making.

"Sorry about that." A man's voice roared over the sound of a still-running chainsaw, hoisted above a felled tree, as he waved at her.

Valerie shielded her eyes from the rising sun, squinting to see the man behind the machine. "Will you turn that off?" As Valerie shifted her weight, the side of her foot caught one of the jagged shards that booby-trapped her. "Ouch!"

Coffee-drenched, skin-pricked, and half-dressed wasn't how she cared to announce herself to the neighborhood of Last Stand.

But the man with the chainsaw and his sidekick hardly looked like neighbors. And the scene that separated them was anything but welcoming.

"What the—"

The rumble of the chainsaw ceased. "At least I didn't hit your car."

Valerie narrowed her gaze on the sawdust-covered imbecile who stepped more fully into view. He was dwarfed by a once towering tree that now lay across her driveway, its heavy limbs narrowly missing her white Kia.

Not only had the tree nearly crushed her only mode of transportation, but its trunk crumpled a line of fine shrubs that were antiques in the rose-growing world, long lived and well loved. She was supposed to meet a real estate agent this afternoon. The plan had been to take exterior pictures of the property, but now the scene was a total wreck, thanks to someone else's incompetence.

Pain shot from Valerie's foot to her head. This was too much to handle. She slammed the door shut, stepping back on yet another ceramic shard that cut again into her skin. She yelled an expletive before limping away from what she hoped was a bad morning dream.

Last Stand certainly wasn't supposed to look like this.

Inside the only bathroom of the century-old home, Valerie stood on her one good foot as she reached into the medicine cabinet and fished for something to take care of her wounds. Her options were an ointment with a yellowing label, a small bottle of peroxide, and a roll of medical tape. She grabbed the peroxide and tape, yanked a thread-bare washcloth from the wall rack, and balanced on the edge of the claw-foot tub as she raised her foot to assess the damage. Two slices crisscrossed her skin in tender places, and both were bleeding.

Maybe this isn't going to be the best idea. Barely clearheaded from lack of coffee yet light-headed at the sight of blood, Valerie unscrewed the bottle and poured a stream of liquid across her foot. Worse than any beverage scald or a vaccine needle puncture, the sting into open flesh made her clench her teeth and toss her head back in a wave of pain.

Don't pass out. Don't pass out.

She'd end up backward in the tub if she did, and then what? Who but a couple of strangers with a chainsaw and a rope outside her door would find her? It all seemed like a horror flick gone completely wrong.

Valerie inhaled a deep breath for strength as she powered through her impulsive method of first aid. She grabbed the washcloth, placed it against the cuts, and lassoed the medical tape around her foot. She leaned down, bit the tape between her teeth to tear it, and secured the slack end against the edge of the cloth.

"There." She extended her foot, appraising the bulky makeshift bandage that at least stopped the bleeding. The skin on her legs was still speckled with coffee droplets, drying to a cakey coating. She rubbed her palm down the length of one, wishing the caffeine could somehow seep into her pores and stir her to think more clearly. There was still the problem of the yard turned upside down, not to mention a couple of crazies blocking her exit.

"Hello?" A loud voice called from the front entrance followed by a triple knock. "Are you in there?"

"You have got to be kidding me," Valerie mumbled, her nerves unraveling as fast as her patience. She was used to apartment living in San Antonio where her neighbors were mostly working professionals who kept to themselves. They were friendly but didn't interfere by bothering, inquiring—or knocking three times on a door they saw was closed.

"I didn't mean to come so close to your car. I'll fix that."

Apparently, this day was out of her control by a country mile. This person wasn't leaving without a face-to-face exchange. Valerie hobbled to the door, tiptoeing around the pieces of coffee mug and its caramel-colored remnants. She swung the door open only wide enough to eye the intruder, but she stayed protectively behind the jamb.

"Don't come in."

"I had no plans to," he countered. "I'm an outside guy."

She could care less for his personal preferences. She might have no use for this tiny slice of real estate she inherited in a place that wasn't home, but she still had every intention of taking care of it until the deed was transferred to a new owner and her sale money was in the bank.

"From where I'm standing, you don't seem to have a handle on outside work. If you did, someone else's tree wouldn't be in my yard."

"I'm sorry about that." The man made a slight motion forward as he continued, "That's why I'm—"

"Don't step there!" Valerie's hand shot between them, willing him to stay put. Jagged pieces of her grandmother's mug lay spread like ashes across a dull and dusty tile floor.

The man followed Valerie's gaze downward before his eyes landed on his footwear. "Good thing I've got my steel toes."

Was that a joke? There was nothing she liked about this

guy. Not his humor. Not his shoes. And not his gruff morning intrusion into her otherwise quiet life.

The man's gaze slid to Valerie's foot. "What happened to you?"

"You really want to know?" Valerie's tone dripped with sarcasm.

She would rather not be spending her precious two weeks of vacation in the middle of nowhere, cleaning, sprucing, and getting an old bungalow ready for sale. But she was. The last thing she needed were interruptions.

The man held up both hands in mock arrest, taking a step backward. "My bad."

That's an understatement.

He lowered his hands but wouldn't back off the impromptu inquisition. "Are you okay?"

"Peachy," Valerie deadpanned.

He shifted his weight. "Maybe you should wear boots around here. Because if you haven't noticed—"

There was a lot Valerie was noticing.

"Rural Texas can be full of surprises."

"Roger that." Valerie wanted to bite back with something far more intense. But even she was a woman with restraint.

Then, as if nuisance knew no bounds, he still didn't leave. On the contrary, the man extended his hand with a smile that signaled a fresh approach. "I'm Hutch."

Even through the situational fog, Valerie's manners drove her response. Her parents didn't raise a brat, and her grandmother had taught her that kindness was never out of style.

"I'm Valerie." Their firm handshake would have seemed normal had it not been for the circumstances involving her yard, her foot, her ruined breakfast beverage, and her bathrobe.

She was still in a barely there robe.

Oh, dear.

Graces aside, she'd never be caught dead meeting someone at her door looking like she did at this moment. But in the throes of upheaval, her attire wasn't a contributing factor in her split-second reactions.

"Hi, Valerie." Hutch's voice was easy. The way he echoed her name sounded like notes of a quick-syllabled song that held none of the grit she'd experienced in their inaugural exchange from far away. Up close, he was almost suave.

Or maybe it was still too early in the morning to think straight.

She slackened her grip and drew back her hand. She wrapped both arms around herself, as if a self-hug would somehow make Hutch ignore the fact that she was in a bathrobe.

Instead, it seemed to draw his attention with a gaze that lingered a beat too long. Valerie cleared her throat.

"I'm going to get that tree cleaned up for you."

"Good." Because that certainly needed to happen. She was a prisoner in the bungalow until that tree was moved.

"Don't worry a thing about it." He placed his left hand against the doorframe as he leaned in closer.

But Valerie was worried. Should she call the agent and cancel? No, this was Hutch's fault, and he needed to make this right. "What about my plants?"

Hutch peered over his shoulder as if the front yard could give its own response. "Brody and I will figure out something. Trust me."

All Valerie had were Hutch's words, and they were in contrast to his bumbling actions. Still, she didn't know anyone in town. "Fine."

Hutch raised his chin, his steely eyes appraising her. "Now, I must say, I'm a little worried about you and that foot."

If there was one thing Valerie could do, it was take care of herself. She had for years. "I'm fine."

Hutch tilted his head, challenging her automatic response. "Let me know if you're not. I'll be out here."

"Working." The single word was a prompt that sounded a bit like a question. Priority one was removing that monstrosity from the driveway.

"That tree will disappear before you can say what," Hutch said.

Valerie rolled her eyes. She wouldn't fall for a silly semantics game of repeating *what*. She eased the door closed as Hutch stepped back. The last image she saw was of him tipping his head in gentlemanly courtesy.

Chapter Two

"BE GLAD THERE wasn't a fence between the properties." Brody congratulated Hutch on his quick thinking.

"Not here in the front yard." Hutch and his only fellow tree trimmer for the day stood on the property line between Valerie's bungalow and that of Mrs. Lydia Lang, a longtime Last Stand resident whose corner lot held a grove of gorgeous post oaks Hutch hated to see go. But Hutch's entrepreneurial mind knew how to take lemons and make lemonade. Even a rotted post oak would have a second life once Hutch got a hold of it.

Post oak was king in The Hut's barbeque pits. Its wood produced smooth smoke that resulted in a rich flavor. Hutch was a true disciple of post oak, just like his grandfather and his father.

Cole, however, wanted to add pecan and mesquite into the rotation, a cardinal sin as far as Hutch was concerned. Such pitmastering tomfoolery would happen over Hutch's dead body. And the way he and Cole had been fighting lately, one of them might just end up in that state.

Hutch shook his head, shaking away the contentiousness that hung like a veil between him and his only sibling. He needed to focus on the tree, which wasn't going to saw itself.

"Let's get this broken down." Even just looking at the tree, Hutch could practically taste the bounty of slow-grilled barbeque treasures it would create. Good barbeque started with good wood.

And the trees of Last Stand, like everything else in the community he loved, were good.

Brody was recoiling the rope they had used for portions of their trim. They'd now need only the chainsaw and their arm strength to cut the wood into haulable pieces. "By the way, did you see where the dog went?"

"Sure didn't." Hutch's specialty was knowing barbeque, but he had also been trimming trees for years. He knew enough about gravity to have taken the gamble on the tree hitting Valerie's driveway rather than the alternative, which he still shuddered to think about. "It was a close call not to hit Nod."

"You think he ran back home?"

"Probably." Hutch waved his hand in a vague direction farther down a side street. "Nod wouldn't hurt a thing," he said of the pet taken in by a barbeque customer he knew. Hutch had once asked about the name Nod; the owner said he was a stray who had shown up for several days in a row. His routine prompted the homeowner to repeat "Not our dog" each time, hoping the canine would find his way somewhere else.

But animals had their own ways of doing things.

Determined to ease his way into the family, the loveable pooch persisted, and the resident's soft heart finally made a home for the stray. "Not our dog" became "Now our dog." Both phrases resulted in the acronym NOD, so that was what the dog was called. "Nod is probably well on his way home." Just a couple of houses away.

City folks used dog leashes, but they were optional in the country. Throughout these sleepy streets where everyone knew everyone, free-roaming Nod was just part of the neighborhood. And in that split second when Nod chose to run under Mrs. Lang's tree, Hutch whacked a quick crosscut he hadn't originally intended into the trunk.

Physics lessons in high school turned out to be good for something.

Had the tree fallen on Nod, Hutch couldn't have lived with guilt of what might have been. Luckily, the dog was fine, and Valerie's car was spared. Still, there was collateral damage to the landscaping.

"You see that?" Brody pointed to the very spot Hutch was contemplating.

Hutch could handle trees, but plants and flowers weren't his wheelhouse.

"I see it." He studied the crushed blooms and flattened bushes. He'd have to do something about those. "Know where we can get some replacements?"

"I've got a vague idea." Brody always did. That was a strong quality of his longtime friend. He was an idea man. In fact, it had been Brody who often found jobs of trimming where the wood was ripe for the pits. Thus, Hutch didn't have to do any advertising. He and Brody could usually manage most jobs, which left Cole with more time at the barbeque market. Time on his hands probably explained all of his wild ideas for wanting to change what had worked for decades in serving customers at The Hut.

Still, as much as Hutch didn't like change when it came to the family business, he was sensible enough to keep his eyes on anything that would increase traffic and generate profits. The older he got, the more his thoughts bent toward the business's bottom line.

The market had been started by their grandfather, who built a reputation on serving quality food to all the hungry carnivores in this part of the Lone Star State. Keeping the pits fueled and overhead costs low were priorities Hutch needed to master in order to keep a strong tradition alive through The Hut. But compromising on post oak wood wasn't an option.

Brody slung the rope over his shoulder as he prepared to stow it back inside the pickup they used for transport. "By the way, was that woman who answered over there in a bathrobe?"

Hutch might have been preoccupied with smoothing over a sticky situation when Valerie swung open her front door, but he still noticed her curves beneath a short, tightly cinched robe held together by a single tie at the waist. "She sure was." Heaven help him, he might have been a man who knew enough to apologize to a woman whom he had surprised, but he was still a man whose red-blooded urges stretched far beyond just barbeque.

VALERIE STILL COULDN'T start the day off on the right foot.

And that might have been because her foot wasn't exactly cooperating with the rest of her body.

She limped back into the kitchen, putting awkward pressure against her heel with every step. She wasn't in much pain, not the physical kind anyway. More the mental crush of when plans didn't pan out the way a person intended.

On the bright side, she didn't have to walk far.

The bungalow's kitchen nearly doubled as the front entrance anyway. The old home was big on charm but not on space. Sure, there were features that would make buyers swoon, like a dropped farmhouse sink, a wood stove in the living room, and wainscoting that had come back into style. But the creature comforts Valerie craved—brisk lighting, storage space, easy-to-reach electrical outlets—were seriously lacking.

So even at its best, the property didn't tug at Valerie's heart.

She just hoped it would for someone else. Because by tearing down drab curtains, repainting the rooms, and repositioning some of the pieces of existing furniture, her hope was to freshen the place enough to attract buyer interest. Then, small touches like reviving the wood on the front door, changing out the drawer pulls in the kitchen, and adding lush bathroom accessories might just ignite enough visual appeal to stir buyers into making an offer.

That was certainly the end game.

Valerie needed a buyer for the house. Staying in Last Stand wasn't an option. Her full-time job, which she adored as much as her lifestyle, was in San Antonio. As an organic grocery buyer for a fast-growing chain of stores, she had charted a professional path, making decisions that mattered, but she didn't need to leave the comfort of the city to make them.

Last Stand made her feel like a fish out of water.

And by the looks of the people she knew of so far—an elderly widow next door and a bumbling tree trimmer who couldn't properly calculate a cut to respect her property line—she wasn't too thrilled with the people of Last Stand.

As long as someone else is. This place wasn't home.

Her parents, who moved around a lot with her father's job, had landed in Kentucky several years ago. When Valerie visited, she saw the best of Kentucky, but outside of horse farms and bourbon distilleries, it was just another location to her.

Although born in Texas, she'd spent only two summers in Last Stand with her paternal grandmother. Memories washed in and out of those times, but she had stopped visiting her grandmother as a preteen, and she never really reconnected as an adult.

Valerie ran her finger across the length of the counter. Decades ago, she could barely see over the lip of its edge as she tried to sneak a taste of her grandmother's molasses cookie batter. She closed her eyes, trying to capture more of the memory, but aside from a mental sepia-colored scene, she could recall little else.

Valerie opened her eyes and stared at the surface, worn from years of use. Her pang of nostalgia should have pulled harder, as she was her parents' only child, just as her father was an only child. She, then, was the lone Perry descendant. As such, her grandmother left what was in the bank to her father and what was on the land to Valerie.

But aside from brief, decades' old memories that could

have been anyone's childhood, any specific connection to this place felt so distant to her. And what would she do with a bungalow in such a place? Her parents had mentioned perhaps she could rent it for a while as extra income, but Valerie didn't want to add landlord to her list of responsibilities, especially for the little bit she could earn in such a rural location. No, selling was best.

The decision was permanent with a known outcome. Valerie liked those kinds of choices.

She grabbed a small notepad on which she had written a list of around-the-house improvements when she walked the interior yesterday evening upon first arriving. She was no renovation expert, which was why her list included easy cosmetic fixes she hoped would be small on cost and big on impact.

Today's agenda involved a visit to the hardware store and a one o'clock visit from a real estate agent who was interested in listing the property. Luckily, the agent was meeting her, but she doubted the hardware store made house calls. She needed her car, but as she pushed back the curtain in the picture window above the sink to peek outside, all she saw was—him.

Him and that stupid chainsaw.

As big and as obnoxiously loud as it was, it still wasn't slicing through the trunk of the downed tree as quickly as it needed to in order to clear room for her to back the car up. Plus, there was a full canopy top to the side whose spindly, half-dead arms stretched dangerously close to the side of her Kia. If she dared to open the trunk or a side door, she'd likely scratch its paint.

So many worries. So much to do. And all of it hinged on some stranger named Hutch's ability to slice, stack, and stow a part of Mother Nature that wasn't even part of Valerie's property.

"YOU WANT ME to go let princess over there know that her driveway is clear?" Brody waved two fingers in the direction of Valerie's front door.

Hutch huffed. Valerie had been surprised by their work and he understood that. He hadn't initially knocked on her door because he had no reason to believe they'd be using her yard as a landing pad for Mrs. Lang's post oak. But sometimes circumstances—make that the actions of one neighborhood dog—required other plans.

"I'll do it." It was only fair that, since delivering bad news, he could deliver a bit of good to Valerie. Not that her front yard was back to normal.

Far from that, actually, as Hutch surveyed the current scene.

But she'd at least be able to get the car out of the driveway if she needed. That was a start. The flattened plants and decorative stone paving that had cracked under the weight of the tree's fall would take time to repair. "This way, I can tell her about that." He pointed to a crack that looked like a lightning bolt cutting across the flagstone.

"Oh, boy." Brody scrubbed his hand over his face. "Are we gonna have to fix that?"

"That would be the right thing to do." Sweat from manual labor, and maybe a dose of anxiety, manifested in tiny beads across Hutch's forehead. He pulled a bandanna from his back pocket and wiped it across his skin, sawdust residue sliding across his facial creases like a crude exfoliator. "I can pick up some filler after my shift. Maybe some sand too. Looks like the stone could use a little bit of leveling anyway."

"I can't help you with that. Not today."

"I know."

Hutch didn't expect him to. His family paid Brody by the hour for tree-trimming assistance, and they worked on the fly. Whenever someone called, they went. There might be back-to-back jobs and then no calls for weeks. Hutch's responsibility was to the barbeque market, but completing jobs like this was still part of what he considered his duty.

Sometimes Cole would help, but it was best they didn't work hand in hand too much. Lately, when they did, they argued. At least with a friend like Brody, they respected one another's habits and just worked until the job was done.

"It's not a problem," Hutch assured Brody. "I'll take care of it." Hard work wasn't everyone's taste, but Hutch loved it. Working with his hands felt primal and good. Sourcing from the land and using natural resources to create food that would nourish his friends and neighbors was his calling.

"I'll load up these branches while you deliver the news to princess." Brody gestured again toward the bungalow. "Besides, she'll be glad to know her precious vehicle doesn't have a scratch. Who drives one of those foreign models around here anyway?" he mumbled. "Seems silly when there's perfectly good American mechanics right here. Don't even know how she gets somebody to work on that."

"It's probably new enough that she doesn't need a mechanic." Which was the opposite of Hutch. He had only ever driven one vehicle, and that was his blue pickup that already qualified as old when he got it. It had been his grandfather's, who drove it until he passed away. The funeral took place when Hutch was in high school. Now, a decade later, the truck was still running, even if it did need mechanical TLC now and again.

Hutch folded his bandanna in half, reached around to his back pocket, and pushed the fabric inside just enough so that it would stay put. His second encounter with Valerie Perry couldn't be any more surprising than his first, unless she answered the door in a bath towel instead of a robe. That would turn his day upside down.

"Wipe that goofy grin off your face," Brody coached, "and go talk to that girl. I haven't got all day."

Hutch strode to the bungalow's front entrance, this time less sheepishly. Now, he was a bit cooler under the collar walking up on his own terms—even if he was hot as heck and probably looked like he had just been pulled from the underbelly of a barbeque pit.

He triple knocked before stepping back to give the woman some space. He was here to deliver good news, not bad. But as Valerie opened the door again, Hutch's smile turned to near delirium.

She wasn't in a bathrobe.

She was in cutoff shorts and a work shirt tied at the waist, leaving a little sliver of skin peeking out from right above perfectly curved hips.

"Yes?" Valerie prompted, forcing his gaze away from her

midsection.

He made eye contact, but that also made him tongue tied. Her hair was pulled back into a messy-sexy bun, little tendrils of loose strands falling into a face that Hutch could have stared at for hours.

"You have more chaos to tell me about?"

Correction. He could have stared had she not opened her mouth.

The reality of the woman before him was one who was short tempered, fussy, and didn't mince words. "Actually . . ." Hutch found his voice through parting mental clouds. "I have good news."

"Shoot."

If her one-word reply held any double meaning, Hutch didn't have the head space to decipher it. "The trunk's gone. You can move your car now."

"Oh, you want me to move my car? Because it's an inconvenience to you and your intrusive operation at the moment?"

Hutch straightened his posture. Such a feisty comeback. "No. Not, um, not unless—"

"Not unless you give me permission?"

"No. That's not, well, what I meant was—"

Valerie cut in again. "Sorry." She then started to say something else but winced before the words came.

Hutch's concern shifted. "Are you okay?"

"Fine."

She didn't look fine. She still wore a rudimentary cast on her foot, and her face was etched in pain.

"You're blowin' smoke." Time to cut to the chase. "Do

you need something for that foot?"

Her voice softened, her demand simple. "I need a proper bandage. I think I'm making it hurt worse by limping around on the heel."

"Brody!" he called over his shoulder without missing a beat. "Get the first aid kit from my glove box."

"You carry a first aid kit?"

"I know it might not be part of the package when you buy a car from some city lot." He couldn't resist a bit of a dig. "But in Last Stand, folks have to be prepared."

"Is that what you call how you operate?"

"Call it what you want." He turned back to see Brody making his way toward where they stood, small metal box in hand. "But, in this moment, I have what you need."

"In this moment. *Only*," Valerie underscored.

"Do you want a bandage or not?"

Valerie's voice softened. "Maybe two, if you have them?" She added a sweetened, "Please?"

"Now, how could I resist such a damsel-in-distress request?" He smiled chivalrously.

Valerie mumbled, "I'm not a damsel."

But Hutch let it go. He thanked Brody, made swift introductions between the two, and popped open the top of the kit. "Your wish is my command." He procured two bandages, holding them to her like a pair of tickets to a palace ball.

She accepted them with a quiet "thank you."

As far as Hutch was concerned, those words were victory in smoothing over what had been a tense morning between them. "It's the least I can do for the a.m. inconvenience."

"I'm probably setting myself up for a week of inconvenience." Valerie sighed, her voice heavy. She didn't make eye contact, her focus and her attention now shifting far away. "I have so much to do."

His best choice would be to keep his end of the conversation light. "Good thing you know a couple of locals." He pointed a thumb at Brody and then at himself.

The line solicited what Hutch thought was the hint of a smile, though, admittedly, the arc of Valerie's lips was hard to read. She might be a good Texas hold 'em player if she could manipulate her face like that.

Still, she piggybacked on Hutch's line. "So locals can direct me to the best hardware store? And maybe a good place to get some lunch?"

Now this woman was speaking his language. "For sure," he promised. He exchanged a knowing smile with Brody.

"I need paint and some other house supplies."

"There's a place that's got that."

Valerie's eyes flashed. "Where is it?"

"Down from the fire station." Brody shared directions to the town's one-stop shop when it came to everything a homeowner needed. "It's called Nailed It."

Valerie chuckled. "Clever."

"Now, when it comes to food," Brody wizened, volleying the conversation. "Hutch knows of an especially good place."

"I'm a picky eater," Valerie began.

But Hutch had heard that before. "Nonsense. The place you should go has things on the menu no one can resist."

"Maybe. Maybe not." Valerie shrugged. She seemed to be running through responsibilities in her mind, her fingers tapping in slight enumeration against the skin of her thigh. "I'll barely have time to eat today."

"No worries." Hutch was not to be deterred. "Stop by this place called The Hut. I'll meet you there, and the meal will be on me. It's the least I can do for all the trouble this morning."

Brody jumped in with quick directions. "On Main Street. You can walk there from Nailed It."

"You'll be in and out in no time."

Valerie looked from Hutch to Brody and back again. Even if she was unsure about the swift litany of foodie talk, she did oblige with, "Thanks for the offer."

Making things right with Valerie became a priority. "I wouldn't steer you to just any place."

"That's really thoughtful, but between my errands and making it back here for pictures with the real estate agent, I won't have a lot of time."

Hutch insisted. "Not a problem. It's practically an institution in the town. I promise it will be a satisfying meal with quick service."

Valerie wrapped one hand around her stomach. "Considering I haven't had breakfast . . ." His words seemed to be working.

"It's settled then. Enjoy The Hut." He snapped the case shut on the first aid kit. "Maybe you can delay those outside photos by a day?"

Valerie bit her lip. "Maybe."

That answer was good enough for Hutch. He turned on his heel and headed back with Brody to finish their work.

Brody waved goodbye before Valerie disappeared into

the house. Hutch and Brody would soon deliver the wood so Hutch could also work the lunch shift. He'd have a fun exchange with Valerie when she put two and two together and realized The Hut was the family business.

To make it easier for her to get in, out, and on with her day, he planned to round up some of the pit's best in a sampler platter. He could set it aside for her. The special selections were sure to be a hit no matter how picky an eater she claimed to be.

Besides, customer acquisition happened best when it was organic, and Hutch was just making the best of an opportunity that presented itself to introduce someone new to their business. And no matter how long Valerie was in town, if Hutch could make her fall in love with their food that was an addition to the family customer base.

Securing the future of Hutchinson's barbeque market was a responsibility he took seriously, as seriously as he took rectifying a bombshell morning meeting with a woman whose Daisy Dukes and waist-tied shirt he could certainly stand to see again.

Chapter Three

CUSTOMERS WERE ALREADY starting to stream in the front entrance of The Hut when Hutch arrived at ten thirty. The events of the morning had caused him to blow his meeting with Cole, but he'd deal with that later. Right now, there were hungry mouths to feed.

He greeted some of the regulars on his way in, stopping to shake hands and exchange well wishes like a politician at an election rally. As customers waited to make their way through the front door, they had a front-row view to all the outdoor action. They could come right up to the pit, point to their preferred pieces, and start making their plates right there. Why Cole wanted to change this was still lost on Hutch.

"It's about time you dragged yourself in here." Cole balled and tossed a red apron at Hutch's chest before turning his attention back to the pits. "You missed our meeting."

Hutch would explain his delay later. "I'm here now."

"I got this." Cole waved him on without looking up from his work.

Hutch didn't want to work beside him today anyway. He'd be more useful inside where customers got their side dishes, drinks, and paid for their purchases. That was where Hutch usually spent his time.

Over the years, his family had expanded what was once just a roadside pit into an air-conditioned dining room with family-style picnic-bench seating, restrooms, and counter for the cash register. The changes had been big and Hutch's grandfather had originally opposed them. Yet they made all the difference in keeping up with expectations of what people wanted, which wasn't always just meat-centric entrees. They wanted meals.

Eventually, their grandfather came around and embraced the change, and the restaurant ran smoothly in the same manner. His mother even added two homemade desserts: hot peach cobbler and cold banana pudding. Those complemented the daily side dish offerings they advertised on their chalkboard menu: potato salad, coleslaw, and . . .

"Corn casserole?" Hutch nearly choked on the words.

"Cole!" He made a beeline for the pits. He cracked his knuckles as he strode back outside, ready to wring his brother's neck.

Every muscle in his body stiffened, and when he went around to Cole's side of the pit, he turned his back on customers so they wouldn't hear his seething. "What is that I just saw inside?"

"I don't know. What did you see?"

"A new menu item." Hutch clenched his teeth so hard that his words barely had any room to escape his lips. "Not approved."

Cole mopped sauce across a wide rack of ribs, as if he didn't have a care in the world. "You know my morning started at four thirty?"

Adrenaline coursed through Hutch's veins with more

AUDREY WICK

heat than what their pits were releasing. "What does that have to do with anything?"

"Five o'clock." He kept his voice low and his tone firm. "Every morning. Right here." He put down the mopping sauce brush, grabbed a couple of ribs by their bones, and presented them on butcher paper to a customer. "Enjoy."

Hutch spun and tried to rearrange his face into something that resembled service with a smile.

"These pits don't run themselves," Cole insisted, using an adage their father had drilled into them from a young age. The hand-built pits, seasoned from years of use, were a source of family pride and were part of the secret to the tastes that kept customers coming back again and again.

Along with an undisclosed recipe for sauce. And The Hut's spice medley in the brisket rub. Plus the perfect beef-to-pork ratio for their specially ground sausage links that hit all the right protein notes.

Hutch could think about barbeque all day long. He nearly did. Which was why he cared so much about the business.

And then there was Cole with his ridiculous ideas. "Talk less. Work more."

Hutch willed himself to take a deep breath. He wasn't one to usually take marching orders from his younger brother. But the line of customers was getting too long to ignore. He slipped on his apron and got to work.

"Pull those two briskets out." Cole nodded in the direction of the smoker. "They're ready to cut."

Hutch slid into a routine he could do in his sleep. He pushed his hands into thick silicone mitts before lifting the briskets, holding their weight like a prize. He placed them one at a time on thick wooden cutting boards that were as old as he was.

Slowly, he unwrapped the butcher paper that blanketed the meat. The smell of barbequed perfection rose on steaming wisps of heat.

Some folks wrapped beef brisket in aluminum foil to smoke, but for years, Hutchinson's had been using simple, old-fashioned butcher paper. The slick inside retained the juices and created a natural baste for the brisket, yet the material still allowed the meat to breathe. This pitmastering technique resulted in a delicate balance of smoke intake from the grill, which underscored the flavor while softening the meat, yielding fork-tender threads that melted in customers' mouths.

Brisket was Hutch's favorite. And with such good reason.

As with a chainsaw, he also knew how to make the most of cuts with a knife—much better than Cole, who always rushed the process. That was something Hutch never did.

Slow and easy. Hutch coached himself to focus, then grabbed one of several trusty electric knives kept at the ready. The knife, small but mighty, revved its concentrated power like a miniature chainsaw. Hutch brought its serrated edge down against the meat, cutting against the grain, which was how every pro cooker worth his salt in the state of Texas did things.

Hutch knew customers wanted the inside to be juicy but the outside to hold a crisp, smoky bark. The interplay was what contributed to the taste. Cutting was as much of an art as cooking to get each quarter-inch slice just right.

"Push five pounds of that aside for a pick-up at eleven."

Hutch nodded to show Cole he heard him as he worked steadily. It wasn't uncommon for customers to order meat by the pound to take with them. It was easy to take the meat straight from the pit, wrap it up, weigh it, round to the nearest dollar, and pass it along to the customer. They kept things simple with white liners and unmarked brown paper bags so as not to fuss with stuffy packaging or specially printed containers.

In fact, nothing about Hutchinson's barbeque market was stuffy. And that was exactly why The Hut was successful.

Hutch would put in a good hour during their busiest time, which was always the shy side of the lunch hour. People came early for the best selection. By noon, the place would be rolling along until they sold out of meat. They didn't keep signage to advertise open hours for that very reason because whenever they did sell out, they simply locked their doors, flipped their sign to *closed*, and started all over the next day.

Hutch kept his eye on the most perfect cuts to set aside for Valerie, snagging four ribs, a sausage link, and some brisket, crowning the gristly edge of one of the cuts atop the stack of marbled slices, spice side up. The Hut's brisket really was king.

Valerie's going to love this. Hutch couldn't wait to see the look on her face.

When there was a break in customer traffic outside, Hutch ducked inside where his mother was working the register and his father was serving sides. Hutch had packaged the meat for Valerie and put it next to the register. "This is for a woman who should be coming in any minute. She's a new customer."

"Good morning to you too." His mother waved him in as she punched a series of numbers while holding a credit card. The family worked together like a well-oiled machine most days, doing what needed to be done by the book but letting other things slide, like a taste test straight from the pit or an occasional on-the-house meal. "You want me to comp this?"

As Hutch and Cole got closer to taking over the business, their parents put them more and more in charge of decision-making. He couldn't give away food all day long, but this was a special circumstance. "I ran into a little trouble this morning trimming trees."

His mother wrinkled her forehead.

"But it's all taken care of now. This is just to make final amends."

"Noted." His mother relaxed her face and finished a sales transaction just as the door opened with a new wave of customers.

And at the end of the line was Valerie, looking a bit overwhelmed as she stepped into the interior.

Hutch wiped his hands on his apron before untying it and stripping it over his head so he could be a bit more presentable. Still sawdust-sprinkled and now smoke-saturated, he was a walking, aromatic advertisement for the finest barbeque money could buy in all of Texas. It was a scent he wore with pride.

"Valerie," he called her attention to where he stood. "You made it!" He flashed a smile.

But her look of unease told him she wasn't as thrilled by

the place as he expected her to be.

He held out his free hand as he closed the space between them. "Welcome to The Hut."

Her response held little fanfare as she looked from the dining space to the chalkboard and back to him. "All barbeque?"

"The meat's the culinary star of the show here." He made a production of grabbing the sampler platter he had put aside and held it out to her. "And the best of the best is right here."

Valerie's face washed pale, a look of sour response as her nose wrinkled. "What is that?"

Wasn't the smell unmistakable? Maybe she was asking for specifics. "Today we've got pork ribs, beef brisket, and—"

For some men, there were deal breakers when it came to the opposite sex. Some refused certain body types, certain ages, or certain personal styles. Hutch liked to think he was fairly open-minded when it came to preferences, though there was one he didn't understand and didn't care to try.

And Valerie Perry announced herself as one of those, using the words for which Hutch had absolutely no use. "I'm a vegetarian."

His movements came to a screeching halt.

Vegetarian? That was the dirtiest admission one could utter in a barbeque joint. Hutch felt sucker-punched.

Meat was his family's livelihood. Sure, in the food service industry, they dealt with the occasional special request.

Salt free.

Sugar free.

Fat free.

They heard it all, even though the loudest voices were a minority. Most people didn't count calories or care about anything other than taste. Still, for those who asked, his family did their best to accommodate, while staying true to their home-cooked, long-standing menu. In fact, their mother had recently experimented with a diabetic-friendly version of banana pudding. She wanted everyone to be able to enjoy their favorite comfort food.

But a no-meat diet had no place in the world, as far as Hutch was concerned. "Vegetarianism is a nasty word around here."

"That's harsh," Valerie balked.

"What do you want me to say?" Hutch had no script for this kind of exchange.

"Not that," she asserted, blowing out a breath and crossing her arms. "It's cruel to kill animals."

Hutch flashed to the close call with Nod. "In some cases, I can agree with that."

"What are you even doing here?" Valerie changed the subject.

"This is my family's business."

Valerie arched an eyebrow, a cute look for her. "I thought you were a tree trimmer."

"I am."

"But you own a business?"

He directed her to the closest table. He didn't want her to leave, and her face said she was ready to bolt. She had come into their place expecting a lunch. And he didn't have the heart to turn any customer away hungry—even a vegetarian. "Let's sit down over here and I'll explain."

Valerie hesitated. "Can I at least get something to drink?"

Hutch uncovered his manners again. "Sorry." He motioned toward a cooler of old-fashioned sodas in glass bottles next to the self-serve station of sweet tea.

She took a step forward. Progress, as far as Hutch was concerned. "Tell me what you want, and I'll grab it. It's on the house."

Valerie took a few more steps forward, her nose high in the air. But it wasn't from pretentiousness. "Is that peach cobbler I smell?"

The surprise question put him more at ease, lifting the mood and lightening the prior sting to his pride. "My mother claims credit for cobbler so good that it could be a meal unto itself."

Valerie smiled. "Then I definitely have to have some of that."

Chapter Four

V ALERIE WAS STARVED.

And it wasn't her vegetarian lifestyle that was to blame.

Aside from a few sips of coffee, she hadn't eaten all morning. Her insides were already twisting, and while the smell of barbeque made her stomach roil, she also had to get some nourishment into her.

And fast.

She had managed to push the meeting with the real estate agent back a couple of hours, so she had a little wiggle room in her schedule. Still, she needed to economize her time, especially given the challenges in getting the front yard back in shape from the morning's damage. So she didn't want to waste time chasing down a new eatery. Not over the lunch hour. And not when The Hut was so easy to find.

"But there's got to be more here than barbeque and peach cobbler," she insisted.

Hutch motioned with his chin at the colorful chalk menu that listed a small but appetizing array of options that didn't include meat.

Right up my alley. Valerie focused on everything that featured a vegetable or fruit. "Corn casserole sounds good."

Hutch coughed and muttered something Valerie

couldn't understand.

"Everything okay?"

"Sure. Fine. Great."

Valerie still wasn't sure what to make of this guy. But this place did hold the keys to satisfying her hunger. "Can I order from the counter?"

"Just walk right up." Hutch stepped out of her way. "Oh, wait." He reached his hand toward her elbow, and the slight graze of contact made her throat catch unexpectedly. His voice softened with a question that sounded like genuine concern. "How's your foot?"

Valerie tucked her elbow into her waist, forcing distance between her and Hutch. Whatever was fluttering inside of her needed to calm down. She focused on her foot rather than the butterflies in her stomach. "Just surface nicks. The bandages helped."

"Good."

"Plus the embarrassment is healing."

"I've seen you in all forms today."

"Yes." She hadn't expected him outside her home, inside her home . . . or to be here in his place of business. Monday had a way of surprising her.

"Go ahead," he urged, giving her space and time to consider exactly what she wanted.

Ultimately, she asked for a scoop of each of their three main sides on a single plate. Hutch's father obliged with a smile and a swift hand to serve up everything to which she pointed. "Crock pickles and Vidalia sweet onions?" He motioned with serving thongs at the two fresh selections. "Each garden grown."

Now you're talking my language. That sealed the deal. "Yes, please."

Her plate held summery shades of fresh food in an attractive, mouth-watering array.

When she looked back at Hutch, he was mouthing something to the woman at the register. With a smile, she called to Valerie, "My son said this is on the house."

Simple gestures of family made her feel welcome, even in a place that was opposite her usual tastes. "Thank you, ma'am."

"Call me Wanda. Everybody around here does."

She nodded before turning back to Hutch, who had chosen a side table in the dining area for them. It was picnic sized and built for more to join, but unless he had invited friends, it looked like it would be just the two of them.

"Got something good there?"

"I sure hope so," she teased.

"A carnivore and herbivore, dining together. Who would have guessed it?"

Certainly not me. Valerie couldn't have anticipated this day if she tried. "So back to this restaurant. It's yours?"

"My grandfather started it. My parents own it now. I'm third generation, and it's staying in the family." Hutch settled himself then grabbed two napkins, passing one to her. "By the way, will it bother you if I eat this meat in front of you?"

The simple question struck Valerie for its thoughtfulness. "I'll be fine. Thank you."

Hutch picked up a fork. Valerie might have been strained at his actions earlier, but now he was at least attempting to make her feel comfortable. Quiet concern, however it was leveled, impressed her.

And in a place that was still foreign to her, any bit of welcome outreach felt good.

"So, what brings you to Last Stand?"

"Simple question." She forked a bite of corn casserole. "Complicated answer."

"I've got time," he insisted, paving the way for her to reveal whatever she wanted.

And since she was going to share basic details with the real estate agent, she figured it wouldn't hurt to get quick talking points in order and try out the conversation on Hutch. "I inherited this house, but I'm not going to keep it."

She got choked up, not because memories were still green but because she hadn't verbalized the event to anyone in a long time. Her parents had been the ones to clean out the contents of the home after her grandmother's funeral, donating most of her clothes, trinkets, and general belongings. They left basic furniture and accessories for staging. It had stood vacant for six months now, until she could arrange the two-week period off work to devote herself to the DIY renovation.

"So you're Val Perry's only granddaughter?"

"Yes." She rested her fork against her plate. She had never used the shortened form of the name like her grandmother did. "I'm named after her." She lowered her voice, eager to hear about the life of a woman she was still struggling to remember. "Did you know her?"

"In name only." Hutch wiped his mouth with the napkin, a small dab of sauce staining the corner which he folded and lay next to his plate. "I know a lot of names just from growing up here, and I remember hers. She must have been about the age of my grandfather."

"Oh?" Valerie's interest stayed piqued. "When was he born?"

As they swapped generational facts, Valerie learned that her grandmother and Hutch's grandfather likely knew each other.

"So then your grandfather and my grandmother would have been the same age in school," Valerie calculated. "Has he always lived here?"

"Never moved away." Hutch spoke between bites. "Last Stand born and bred, from the cradle to the grave."

That was more history that Valerie could imagine, especially considering her life of moving to half a dozen places before she was a teenager.

"Staying in the same place is sort of standard for the branches of the Hutchinson family."

Now it was Valerie's turn to make a legacy connection. "Hutchinson," she repeated. "Is that why people call you Hutch?"

Her lunch partner shifted in his seat. "You could say so."

Valerie sensed there was more to it than that. They were already having more of a conversation than she expected she would with anyone while she was in town. One-on-ones over lunches weren't her goal during the two weeks she planned to be here. "So what's the full story?"

Hutch stopped eating, holding Valerie's eye contact in a stare down that took her a moment to realize was more alarm than abrasiveness. "That's something people don't ask."

"I'm asking."

"I know."

They continued staring, but something about the exchange spurred her to try an additional angle. "I'm just an out-of-towner. What's the harm in telling me?"

Hutch narrowed his eyes. "Fine." It was as if he was calling draw on their duel of words. "I am actually named after my grandfather."

She had common ground with Hutch in being named after a grandparent. "What's so hard to admit about that?"

Hutch drew a breath. "Because we share a name I don't use."

"And what's that?"

Hutch chewed his lip, tasting the syllables before he released them in one swift and sheepish reply. "Bubba."

Bubba? Nothing sounded more rural than that.

But judging from Hutch's face, he expected her to burst out laughing. Instead, she swerved the other way. "So you prefer Hutch?"

"To that name? For sure." Hutch let go of his fork, scrubbing his hand across his forehead. "Geez, I have no idea why I just told you that." He let out an uncomfortable chuckle.

"Is that not common knowledge around here?" Last Stand seemed small enough that secrets didn't stay hidden for long.

"Around here"—he lowered his hand, resting it against the table top—"locals have strong memories when it comes to some things, short ones when it comes to others. I've been going by Hutch so long that I don't think most people even give it a second thought anymore."

"So no one calls you Bubba?" She kept her tone even and her volume low, the name gliding off her tongue. The roughness of the name melted away, and Hutch seemed to recognize the difference.

"Well, when you say it like that . . ." He looked down at his lap.

And as he did, she swore his cheeks reddened, just enough that the light blush of his skin tone not only softened their conversation but seemed to somehow relax the tough edges of the hapless man she thought was sitting before her.

WITH THE HUM of fellow diners around them and the whir of others going about their business, time passed quickly. Hutch rarely sat in the dining room to eat, but he wanted to show Valerie some small-town hospitality.

In their conversation, she revealed her passion for work, a trait Hutch shared. They also had commonality in being named for a family member, and they shared a love of animals, even if they didn't agree when it came to their diets.

Plus, Valerie was easy on the eyes.

She was in the same sexy outfit as earlier in the day. The thin fabric of her shirt skimmed her curves in all the right places. Even though the long sleeves and button front covered most of her, he had to keep from staring lest he imagine what was just beneath the fabric.

But he had a pretty good idea.

Chenille from a bathrobe, plaid from a work shirt—it

didn't matter what this girl wore. Every look caught his attention, and their conversation stuck with him because just talking about his grandfather for a short time reminded him of the legacy he owed to his name. Hutch needed to get on the same page with Cole, and they needed to stop feuding. Split decisions were no way to run a business.

The time spent together with Valerie was a surprise one-eighty from their off-on-the-wrong-foot morning encounter. There was more to her than met the eye. She knew how to say some of the right things.

"The corn casserole was really good." She stood from their table and licked her lips.

Well, maybe not *all* the right things.

"I'll tell the, um . . ." It took every ounce of restraint Hutch had not to fire back a crude comment about his younger brother. He settled on the word, "chef." Cole had had his little bit of fun by sneaking that onto the menu, but Hutch would put a stop to his shenanigans. Tomorrow, the menu would be back to normal.

Valerie took a few steps forward and waved a jazzy-fingered goodbye. "I appreciate the lunch today, Bubba." She winked, spun on her heel, and let the surprise of her final word trail in her wake.

People didn't call Hutch that. But Valerie seemed to grab permissions on her own accord.

Spunky.

Unexpected.

He liked those characteristics.

Valerie disappeared before he could pick his chin up off the floor—but not before Cole rounded the corner for his own inquisition. "Who was that?"

Hutch didn't want his brother souring an otherwise enjoyable lunch. "A new customer."

"I'll say. I've never seen her."

"Well." Hutch swiped his napkin across his fingers a final time before compacting it into a tight ball, aiming for a spot just inside of the rim of the trash can, and sinking it there in one fluid shot. "Now you have."

"She seemed to like the corn casserole." His lips curled in smug satisfaction.

"Whatever."

"By the way," Cole scoffed, "nice of you to disappear on the job."

"Stopping for twenty minutes on our least busy day of the week to get a plate? That doesn't qualify as a disappearance."

"You sure were getting cozy with her." Cole just wouldn't drop it.

"We were hardly cozy." They dined, after all, in plain sight. He pushed past Cole, shouldering his way right back to work.

"Whatever you say," Cole trailed, his words continuing to grate on Hutch's nerves. His brother was like that. A button pusher who knew how to get under his skin.

Cole called after him. "We need to talk about my plans."

Hutch didn't like the idea of change any more than he liked the idea of vegetarians driving menu changes at the family's barbeque business. Cole shouldn't use one comment from Valerie to justify his underhandedness that flew in the face of what was supposed to be a partnership. "We don't need to talk about those because nothing's going to happen."

"The only way it's not going to happen," Cole insisted, "is if you don't make it happen."

"And I won't make it happen." Hutch stood his ground.

"Hear me out." His voice held a soft plea, sounding more like the younger brother he was. "Just listen to what I have to say this time."

"I'll listen." Hutch could give him that. "But things are running well here." He angled himself behind his brother, placed his hands on his shoulders, and squared his gaze to the heart of the dining area. "Look. Tell me what you see."

"I see old furniture, empty seats, and wasted space."

Not the answer Hutch was looking for.

With the heel of his hand, he popped Cole on the side of his head. "Hey!" He weaved out of Hutch's grasp only to volley. "Tell me what you see."

So much. Hutch took a deep breath, his chest swelling. "I see a family business." He nodded his chin toward a framed black-and-white portrait of Grandpa Bubba Hutchinson centered on the far wall. "A legacy sustained. And a customer base that pays the bills."

"But—"

Hutch held up a single hand. "Later." He brushed his hands together to indicate the conversation was over. "After we clean the pits, I'll listen." He turned and walked away from Cole. It was time to make his own feelings more firmly known because he wasn't going to spend the next ten years wasting energy on passing fads and pointless renovations. Tradition had gotten the family this far, and he wasn't about to destroy everything the family had built.

If there was one thing Hutch valued, it was his family, especially that man whose picture held a constant place in the business and in his heart. Grandfather Hutchinson was the type of man Hutch aimed to be, one who valued hard work, honesty, and steady dedication.

Not change for the sake of change like Cole.

Chapter Five

VALERIE HEADED BACK to the bungalow. As contented as her stomach was, her head was anything but. Surely, the agent was expecting a picture-perfect front yard. And while Hutch and Brody had cleared the driveway, they wouldn't be able to put in plants until later.

"There's always Photoshop," Valerie mused as she waited for the agent to arrive.

She could have listed the property herself on a website, but she was on a time crunch and aimed to maximize her profit with someone professional handling the sale. Besides, she couldn't afford a mistake, and such a big transaction was outside her comfort zone. In her adult life, she had rented apartments and completed lease agreements. But in those cases, all she had to do was sign her name on a dotted line since there was always someone else guiding the process. Here, she wanted to leave no room for error when it came to paperwork.

Besides, her hands were full with necessary updates that would at least bring the home into the twenty-first century. "Oh, Grandma." Valerie sighed as she pushed aside the lace curtains of a large rectangular window overlooking the backyard. The delicate, yellowing fabric was thin as phyllo dough in her hands. "These window dressings probably came with the house," she murmured, running her palm against the fabric and brushing away dust as she tried to uncover memories her lunchtime conversation with Hutch had brought to the surface.

Did these same curtains hang that last summer she spent with her grandmother all those many years ago?

Flashes of remembrance passed through Valerie. Images, mostly. She closed her eyes to see them.

A knife hitting bluntly against a cutting board.

The smell of fresh lemons.

Her grandmother guiding her to squeeze each half above a glass pitcher.

The sting of the juice as it glided across paper thin cuts on her finger pads from dewberry vine scratches that hadn't yet healed.

Valerie willed her eyes open and pulled back. The sensation inside her memory was so real in that moment that she flipped her hand and examined the palm.

Her skin was perfect. Not a cut.

And why would there be? She hadn't done any manual labor in the last twenty-four hours, certainly not to the tune of what Hutch performed.

Hutch. Bubba. A smile played across her lips. That he told her of such a private matter still surprised her. Why did he feel the need? Or was there more to the meaning of their conversation? The new experience mingled in her mind with old memories that she fought to pin down.

But just as easily as thoughts washed in, they washed away.

Making lemonade with her grandmother was a memory.

That was all. And soon, too, would be today. The house. The neighbors. The town.

This house was being sold and Valerie Perry was on borrowed time in Last Stand.

She bit her lower lip and glanced at her watch. The agent would be here any minute. She had written a series of questions on a notepad the night before, and as she turned to retrieve them from the kitchen counter, a knock on the front door signaled Penny Bristo of Bluebonnet Realty.

As Valerie swung the door open with a cheerful "hello," she was steamrolled with a sassy appraisal that wrapped introductions and cut-to-the-chase into one.

"I'm Penny." All Valerie could see of the woman were black sunglasses with lenses the size of cup saucers. "Love the place; hate the curb appeal."

Valerie's mouth hung open like a trout's.

"What happened out there?" Penny stepped around Valerie to invite herself in.

Valerie bristled, her lungs filling with defensiveness.

Which completely surprised her.

Because aside from the tree debacle this morning, she hadn't previously experienced a shred of self-protecting interest regarding the place.

"Looks like a tornado blew through the driveway."

"That would be Hutch."

"Hutch?" Penny lowered her sunglasses to reveal a piercing set of orbs the color of money. Apt, it seemed, for a woman who was billed the top agent in the tri-county area. "As in the barbeque boy?"

Valerie smiled. To be known by such a phrase was the

antithesis of how people in her professional circle referred to others. "I guess he has quite a reputation."

Penny arched an eyebrow that was clearly drawn on that morning. "Was he working for Mrs. Lydia?"

Valerie couldn't remember the name, though she had heard a first and last. "I think so."

Penny pushed her glasses atop her head, a hairspray-slicked, back-combed crown of blonde providing a landing pad for the heavy frames. She reached into her purse and started texting even before her cell phone was fully within view. "Tree removal?"

"Yes." *In a sense.* Although "removal" implied a more careful approach than Hutch seemed to take. "One of the trees sort of crashed across the driveway."

"Sort of crashed?" Penny's head stayed bent over her phone, her thumbs flying across the screen.

Valerie remembered her own quick-tempered response to Hutch this morning.

Before they talked.

Before he helped her with her foot.

Before she ate a complimentary lunch at The Hut.

"Okay," Valerie conceded, brushing aside a full explanation. "He did some debris removal out there, but there's more to be done."

"Got that right."

"He's bringing plants by this afternoon."

Penny's fingers continued to pound away on her phone. "And what about that crack in the walkway?"

"Crack? What crack?"

Penny made a show of finishing her message by striking

her finger dramatically against a final key. "No buyer's going to miss it."

But Valerie sure did.

How?

"I'll show you when we walk the property later." Penny must have read the look of confusion on her face. Penny raised one hand and circled her finger in the air before adding, "Don't let that boy off the hook for his mistake. I don't care if he *is* a Hutchinson."

And that last phrase made Valerie want to turn over the words, prying Penny for clarification on exactly what she meant by them. But her mile-a-minute flurry of activity left little opportunity to interject.

Valerie needed Penny to know how seriously she took this sale. "I want the house in the best shape it can be."

"Well, we agree on that. And for Hutch's part in this, I gave him a deadline of twenty-four hours. He knows better than to leave a yard in disarray."

Valerie, confrontational as she was, wasn't one to criticize a man when he wasn't even here to defend himself. "The yard looks a lot better than it did."

"I'm sure of that." Penny dropped her phone into her purse so large that it doubled as her sidekick. "But, honey, there are standards to meet when it comes to curb appeal. And I hate to break it to you this way, but Hutch may have done you a favor. Those bushes needed to go."

Valerie bristled again. True, she was no master gardener, but the hard-hitting comment still stung. After all, those antique rose bushes were a remnant of her grandmother that Valerie thought were just fine as they were. They were established. In bloom. Certainly having something there beat having nothing at all on that side of the yard.

Penny leveled a simple assessment in the absence of verbal follow-up. "Those type of plants date the house."

"But they're just plants. And Hutch said he's going to replace them—"

"Not with anything similar, I hope."

She wasn't sure but vowed, "I'll take care of it."

"Good." Penny tapped the side of her purse. "I already have several people in mind for this place."

"You do?" Those words were music to Valerie's ears.

"Yes. But I want us to talk about updates before we start expecting offers."

"I agree things could be done to make the atmosphere a little more inviting."

"Good." Penny surveyed the interior with a pleased expression. "I'll type up some recommendations and send them by five o'clock."

Valerie already had her own ideas, but it couldn't hurt to see how they compared to those of a professional.

Penny then performed an interior walk-through, parading in and out of every room like a pageant queen, snapping pictures on her phone as she went. Valerie stepped into the kitchen, basking in the stream of sunlight and trying not to anticipate how many items would ultimately be on Penny's list of necessary updates—and how much everything would cost.

When Penny rejoined her, Valerie said, "I have a limited budget."

"My specialty is to stretch," she said with a wink of an

eye, her skin awkwardly taut from what looked like one too many Botox applications.

To each her own. What women did to their bodies was their choice. Just like, ultimately, what Valerie would do to this home was her choice. She just hoped whatever Penny suggested was practical, manageable, and would make a difference in attracting a high-dollar buyer.

Once she finished with the interior, Penny told Valerie, "Grab your phone." She motioned for her to follow outside. "You might want to take pictures of those hazardous cracks in the stone walkway."

Hazardous?

Valerie hadn't seen anything when she left for the hardware store and lunch earlier. Granted, her attention had been on the large open space that disappointingly resulted in a loss of shade to one side of the yard. Yet, on the positive side, the house seemed a little brighter with the neighboring canopy cover lifted. Had her eyes been looking up and missing what was down?

Bingo.

Tree bark littered the area in pieces like spilled mulch.

Penny brushed the platform of her stiletto across the path, cutting through the debris. "There," she pointed with the toe box. "And there."

Her grandmother's giant flagstone walkway, a quaint and lovely meandering swatch that added a cottage appeal to the place, had a large crack in the most prestigious stone, with several smaller hairline ones in adjacent stones. Jagged shards from the splits lay so close she was lucky to have not rolled her ankle with a misstep.

And these were all fresh cracks.

As in, created this morning.

"Hutch!" Valerie spit his name like a curse word. How could she have been so stupid? The guy had wooed her with a free meal and a promise of plant replacement without ever acknowledging this major fault. Her first instinct had been right. Earthquake-like force did this. But it wasn't the result of a natural disaster. It was the result of a bumbling man.

Now, she had a path that was as much of an eyesore as it was a trip hazard.

Penny mentioned curb appeal, and she was absolutely right about that. Valerie didn't want to give buyers the impression that the ground was shifting beneath the very place they stood when they first got out of their cars.

And she wasn't going to let some local barbeque boy get off easy.

She clutched her cell phone in a palm that grew hot with frustration. "What is Hutch's phone number?"

Better than Google, Penny pinged a digital listing to Valerie's phone that contained Hutch's personal number as well as one for the barbeque market. In the spot reserved for first and last name, Penny had typed "*BBQ Boy One.*"

"That's a much nicer name than I want to call him." Valerie punched a call through to his personal number.

On the second ring, he answered. "Hutch here."

"You cracked my sidewalk."

"Is that a pick-up line?" Hutch's response was immediate, and his laughter rolled through the airwaves.

But Valerie was taking no part in it. "You wish."

"Let's try this again."

"You cracked my sidewalk," Valerie repeated, this time with more force. "And since I'm getting ready to sell a house, I can't have a broken walkway."

"I understand."

"Do you?" Because to her, his voice was lackadaisical, his words empty. "I'm serious."

"I don't doubt that."

This was like talking to a teenager. Maybe Penny's "*boy*" label was exactly right. "Look," Valerie started again. If only she had seen the damage earlier and could have addressed the severity of it when he was still there in person. "I have a limited amount of time here."

"We all do."

That was it. She was about to blow a gasket. "Stop with the philosophical side comments. I can do without those."

"But not with a crack in a walkway?"

"Multiple," she underscored. Penny was counting them on her fingers as she gave a crisp nod. "I'll have you know there are multiple cracks. And I didn't put them there."

"And I did."

"Now we're getting somewhere." Valerie took a breath for perhaps the first time since the start of the call.

"I'll look at it when I bring the new plants by tomorrow."

"Tomorrow? You said today."

"Change of plans. I'll have more time to look at it on Tuesday."

"You'll do more than look at it." Valerie's pulse raced.

"I've got to start somewhere."

"Fine."

"And then I'll have to see about Mrs. Lang's homeowner's insurance and whether or not—"

"Hold it." Valerie's breath was as hot as her temper. "Insurance?"

"Yes. Whatever damage you're seeing might be repairable under a claim."

Valerie once had hail damage to a car. And while it was a relief that insurance would pay for repairs, it was an absolute nightmare of paperwork, delays, and inconveniences to get everything done. Any type of insurance claims would take time that Valerie simply didn't have. "I can't wait for that. This wasn't my fault in the first place."

"Well, technically, it wasn't my fault either because—"

"Enough." She was in no mood for an excuse. "There are cracks in the driveway from a tree that wasn't even part of my property. I want them fixed." She didn't wait for Hutch's response or an exchange of goodbyes. She punched *End* on the call before she said words so unladylike her grandmother would turn over in her grave if she heard them.

All Hutch had to do was take ownership of a mistake, fix it, and move on. Why did men like him have such a hard time doing that?

"You handled that well." Penny stood beside her, but Valerie still felt alone. She stood on inherited property that she never asked for. She wasn't wistful or nostalgic or comfortable. She was annoyed, frustrated, and maybe even in over her head.

She had told her parents she didn't need their help. She'd assured them that she could take care of the sale on her own. After all, she was used to being in control when it came to decisions at work and in her own personal life. Why should closing this chapter in her family history be any different?

Yet, since nothing on her first full day in Last Stand had gone as planned, everything was feeling different. And *different* was exactly the type of curveball she didn't need in her life.

Chapter Six

"YOU LOOK LIKE you just got chewed up and spit out," Cole said.

"Something like that." Hutch was still reeling from Valerie's comments. "Hell hath no fury like a woman scorned."

Cole chortled. "You don't even have a woman."

"That makes two of us."

"I've got some prospects."

Now it was Hutch's turn to chortle. "I'll believe it when I see it."

"Whatever." Cole's dismissive response was more telling of the truth.

"You sure like to talk a big game."

"And what about you? What game are you playing with whoever was on the line?"

"That"—Hutch pointed with one hand to the phone he palmed in the other—"was a new neighbor of Mrs. Lydia Lang."

"You going after widows now?"

Hutch was ready to launch the phone at his brother. "Very funny."

"So, seriously, who was that?" Even Cole's curiosity needed to be satiated. "Is that the girl from lunch?"

"Her name is Valerie." Hutch thought for a moment

about the best way to describe her. "She's kind of feisty."

"That's a quality I always look for in a woman. How old is she?"

If Cole was getting any bright ideas, Hutch was going to put them to a stop with this conversation. "Don't even think about it. She's hard enough for me to handle."

"Then I surely don't want her." He dusted his hands in a show of dismissal. "Besides, I have other things on my mind."

"Here we go." And just like that, Cole flipped a switch from brotherly repartee to restaurateur strategizing. "I ordered some new seating this afternoon."

"You did what?" Hutch's voice rose like an angry parent's. But neither his father nor mother was present. There was no one else in the dining area to referee or mediate.

"Just a couple of tables and chairs." Cole dismissed the major decision as if it were as common as buying ground pepper.

Hutch had so many questions, he hardly knew where to begin. He gulped and managed only one syllable. "Why?"

"Because we need to maximize the space in here."

That was the original reason behind picnic-style seating. It could hold a lot. Hutch scrubbed his hand across his face. He summoned patience he barely had. "Mom and Dad decided on this configuration. And it's worked." Aside from that, they had invested a great deal of money in the eighties on the all-wood setup. The tables had been crafted right here in Last Stand.

"But if we add counter-height stool seating over here with pub-style tables" Cole spread his hands wide as if putting the dining area on theatrical display.

"Hold it." That phrase was a red flag. "No one uses the word *pub* in Texas."

"It's just a design term."

"Oh, excuse me, Mr. Culture." Little brother educating big brother wasn't a game Hutch liked to play. "You learn that term in college?" he jabbed. Neither of them had spent any time in a college classroom.

"I surely didn't learn it by sitting around here. I've been looking online and thinking about the best ways to maximize what we have. Just listen." Cole gassed on about how the setup could accommodate more people when the tables were configured a certain way.

"And what about wheelchairs and strollers?" Plenty of customers came in, after all, needing accommodations for all types of wheeled devices, and picnic tables made it easy to adapt the seating space to those. "Plus, our high chairs won't work with those styles." Hutch pointed specifically to the pub tables.

"Then mamas and daddies don't need to sit there." It was just like Cole to get annoyed at any bit of sidelining. "Look, we get these tables in, and once we rip down all the wood paneling and add sheetrock—"

"Whoa." Hutch held up a hand. "Since when did this turn into a teardown?"

"I'm just thinking down the road."

"Do me a favor. No, do *us* a favor." His hand sliced through the air in time with his words. "Stop. Thinking."

"One of us has to. Because if we don't," he warned, "this place is going to fall into disrepair."

Hutch threw both hands in the air. "You act like we're in some shack."

"That's the thing. I don't want us to get to that point."

It was time for Hutch to put a stop to Cole's one-sided decisions. "This is a partnership. We are in this." He needed to pound teamwork into Cole's hard head. "You can't change the menu. You can't order new furniture. You don't need to fix what's not broken."

"But if it's starting to crack—"

"It's not." But Hutch sure felt like *he* was starting to crack. Which reminded him . . .

Valerie.

The walkway.

He had so much to do but could only focus on one crisis at a time.

"Look," he tried a more didactic approach. "These changes are costing us money."

"But they might just make us money in the long run."

"I knew you would say that."

"Because it's true."

Hutch summoned the strength of an Alamo metaphor Cole might more readily understand. "I'm drawing a line in the sand. Neither of us can make a menu change without the other person agreeing. And neither one of us can authorize orders that aren't from grocery suppliers. Food only. No furniture. No fixtures. No renovation. Not until we run this month's numbers and project costs to take us through the year's end."

Cole narrowed his gaze. "Do you know something I don't?"

Cole hadn't seen the latest property tax bill.

Or the letter from one of their biggest vendors about a freight increase they were passing along to customers.

Hutch wasn't exactly keen on sharing bad news. Yet Cole's shoot-from-the-hip decisions weren't based on the knowledge that Hutch had, so he needed to level with him.

Even when the news was grim.

LATER THAT AFTERNOON, as Valerie was wiping down walls and baseboards in anticipation of new paint, she heard a ping on her cell phone. Penny's message arrived a few minutes shy of her self-imposed deadline.

She's punctual. Valerie conceded that.

She skimmed a finger across her cell phone screen.

And scrolled.

And scrolled.

And scrolled.

If she had been surprised by some of Penny's comments in person, that reaction paled in comparison to her surprise at seeing what she put in writing.

She suggested new paint and window dressings, which were the main part of Valerie's plan. But she added suggestions for new lighting fixtures and faucets, kitchen appliance updates, power washing the exterior, and fresh landscaping.

"What, no kitchen sink?" Valerie chided. The woman had listed practically everything else, including something she didn't even understand.

The words "*stage with a shabby-chic angle*" stared back at

Valerie as boldly as blue eye shadow.

"Shabby chic" wasn't a part of her style repertoire. She knew modern and minimalist, traditional and Tuscan. Coastal, Victorian, French country . . . but she had to google what Penny was suggesting.

She came across several websites on her phone that described shabby chic in varying ways. Some pointed to vintage-inspired designs and an eclectic, quirky mix of repurposed and reconditioned furniture. Some pictures looked Bohemian, some more rustic. Charm was so subjective.

Valerie scrolled through the images that appeared first, growing more confused with each swipe across the small screen. She read captions where she could, because some websites insisted anchors like chandeliers and ornate wall hangings were the cornerstones of pulling a space together, but others mentioned the need for more specific structural elements like crown molding and certain window frames.

Whatever shabby chic was, it was clear the bungalow didn't have it.

Her parents had cleaned out the closets, removed the trinkets, and pared down the contents of the cupboards and shelves to only bare essentials. So when it came to personality and an actual human's footprint of daily life, the house didn't have much.

Which she had thought was perfect for selling the place.

She flipped back to Penny's message, reading the list again.

"Apparently not," she mouthed in surrender, clicking out of the digital windows she had just used. She placed the phone on the counter and stared instead out of the real windows that surrounded her.

Valerie had chosen Penny as her agent from an internet search. Bluebonnet Realty had an easy-to-navigate website, and they listed properties on both a regional and a statewide network online. Still, perhaps Penny's local leads were really going to be her best bet for a sale.

With no one else to lean on, Valerie had to place her trust in Penny. If she thought the market demanded shabby chic, Valerie owed it to her to deliver. After all, she never backed down from a challenge. Especially not when money was on the line. She had one shot when it came to actually selling the place, and she needed to do everything she could on her end to pave the way for making the highest profit possible.

So the next day, she decided an hour of good old-fashioned research was well worth her time. The more she looked online—and the more she drained her data use with roaming charges she didn't care to rack up—the more confused she became. Online, there were almost too many ideas and interpretations when it came to defining décor style.

On her way to The Hut the day before, she'd passed the grounds of the local library. She hadn't paid attention to operating hours, though surely by midday on a Tuesday the place would be open.

Getting a couple of books would give her something tangible to use in figuring out the route to take in transforming the interior into what Penny was after.

Valerie Perry walked into the Last Stand library like a

woman on assignment.

Because she was.

"May I help you find something?" A friendly voice rang through the quiet stacks as she trailed her fingers across the spines of various titles in the architecture section. It was a small collection of books that was nonetheless proportional to the small interior space of the rural library.

"Maybe." She looked up to see a prim, unmistakable librarian smile. But it was attached to a face younger than she expected. "Are you a librarian here?"

"One of them." She nodded, her porcelain features framed by long, smooth strands of red hair that cascaded around a flowy infinity scarf Valerie thought was quite stylish. "Last Stand is lucky enough to have two."

Two librarians. She was used to metropolitan libraries of several stories and an army of workers and volunteers. This place was the size of a bookstore.

And not even a big bookstore.

In the absence of a reply, the woman held out her hand. "I'm Quinn."

Valerie reciprocated with her name, but the formality of shaking hands with another woman who looked to be her own age seemed odd.

"Are you looking for something in particular?" Quinn released her hand and squared her stance in front of the books. "I may be able to help."

"I could use some help," Valerie confirmed. *In more ways than you'd probably guess.* "I'm looking for some books on interior design. Specifically, I need to know more about shabby-chic design."

"I can help with that." Quinn's confidence was as swift as her movements. She sidestepped two rows to her right and pointed to a shelf. "There are a couple of books here in the seven forties on decoration and interior design." She grabbed two books that were night and day different, one a thick hardback volume and one a thin paperback with full-color glossy photographs.

Valerie pointed to the second. "That looks like it might have some good ideas."

"Are you looking to replicate the style?"

"I think so." As Quinn passed the book to her, Valerie quickly explained the current state of her life in the middle of a real estate affair. "So I'm trying to woo potential buyers and also make the agent happy enough that she had reason to push the property."

"I see."

Valerie hoped she wasn't oversharing, but it was nice to talk through the situation with someone. Verbalizing the process in broad strokes helped her visualize the steps before her more clearly.

"From what I know about shabby chic, folks want feminine colors, soft textures, and delicate touches." Quinn's statement was clearer than any Valerie had read online; she could immediately see those aspects in her mind.

"Go on," she urged, stilling her fingers from flipping through the book's pages as she focused on Quinn.

"Well . . ." Quinn looked momentarily at the space above Valerie as if choosing which ideas she wanted to share next. "For the color palette, think whites, creams, and pastels."

"I can work with that."

"Sweet and cozy pieces are really the key to mixing and matching."

It started to click. Valerie had seen that in the varying pieces of worn-out furniture staged in online showrooms the night before. "But one part is still giving me trouble."

"What's that?"

"What some people consider charming, I consider tasteless."

Quinn laughed and kept her voice low, as if the two were sharing a secret. "I know what you mean. There's a fine line."

Valerie flipped through the pages of the book. "See? Like this." She opened the book wide and held it out for Quinn to see. She pointed to a frou-frou vanity. "How am I supposed to accomplish that in a century-old bathroom?"

"You have a century-old bathroom? Where did you say the house is located?"

Valerie hadn't. But she shared the address with Quinn.

"I know where that is." Why did that line not surprise her? Everybody probably knew everyone else's business in a place like Last Stand. "Is there a claw-foot tub?" Valerie nodded, and Quinn practically cooed.

"I'm glad somebody likes the idea of one of those. At least I won't have to replace that."

Quinn gasped like Valerie had personally offended her. "You better not replace a perfectly good claw-foot tub."

Quinn had more of an attachment to the idea than Valerie had to the reality of it. "Well, I won't be able to do this type of design in there." She pointed again to the page.

"But if you have features that are original to the house, you have exactly what you need to build around and easily create something fabulous." Quinn's enthusiasm was so torrential it nearly spilled over into Valerie.

Nearly.

Valerie shut the book. "If I take this, I may be able to get some more workable ideas."

"You can take it," Quinn agreed, "but it's better if you check it out instead." She smiled. "Library humor."

It wasn't that funny. But Valerie wasn't about to say so. Quinn was kind, and Valerie appreciated her help with finding a great book. She told her so.

"It's why I'm here. And why librarians are still important," she added a quick plug for her profession.

"Have you been a librarian long?" Valerie followed Quinn as she led the way to the circulation desk.

"Just hired this year." Quinn's facial reaction as she turned back to Valerie was sheer delight. "It's my first full-time job."

She could relate to that feeling. "Congratulations on that."

"Thank you." Quinn continued moving forward but spoke so Valerie could still hear. "I'd love to know how everything turns out. And if you need a second set of eyes to make decisions, I'd be happy to give it a shot."

"That's not a bad idea." Her reply was immediate, as much of a reaction to all she had to do as well as her current uncertainty about how, exactly, to do it. "If you're serious—"

"It would be fun to help." Quinn didn't miss a beat. As

she slid around to the other side of the desk, she bent her head and admitted quietly, "It's nice to chat with someone my own age in here for a change."

Valerie looked around. Aside from a few children and their parents, the majority of people using the facilities at this time of day were elderly. They did appear to be the only people in the library in their midtwenties.

"By the way"—Quinn tapped a key on the edge of the computer's keyboard to wake up the machine—"do you have a library card?"

"For this library? No, actually."

"Not a problem." Quinn started typing and said, "I'll get you set up with one right here."

Valerie certainly didn't have plans to be a library patron beyond this one instance. She hadn't even intended to check out a book. She'd figured if she did find something worth considering, she'd simply take some photos with her phone or pay for a few copies of select pages.

Although, now that the book was in her hand, being able to peruse it at her leisure and in the comfort of the actual space she was going to be transforming was a much better idea anyway.

Quinn seemed all too pleased to be able to tally a new user for the library. "I'll print a card and laminate it for you. Carrying it, you'll feel just like a local."

Valerie highly doubted that would be the case. If there was one thing she didn't want to be confused about, it was a long-term association with Last Stand. Her life was in San Antonio, and after she took care of what she needed, she'd be back there with only memories of this place in her rearview mirror.

Still, Valerie could use a friend, if only for the short-term. "Thank you." She accepted the card from Quinn, whose smile and kindness put her at ease.

Already, Valerie felt more in control than she had in the previous day. It was a simple outreach. She sought help for something she didn't understand and she received it. She did that in her professional life, so now she just needed to get comfortable doing that in her personal life. Because happy results might just be worth their extra effort.

Chapter Seven

HUTCH POINTED TO a bush without an identifying marker. "What's that called?"

"How am I supposed to know?" He and Brody were out of their elements at the one place they could think of to get plants to replace what they had flattened in Valerie's yard. It was an unmarked sales location in a home that doubled as commercial space. Owned by a local, of course, plants of all varieties were grown and available for sale whenever the owner happened to be there.

Which was pretty frequently. She was a friend of Lydia Lang's and had to be her age, which was eighty. Or more. When women hit the upper decades, it was hard to tell.

"Isn't there a Popsicle stick in some of those?" Hutch bent to get a closer look, searching for the simple marker on which the plant names were scribbled to help identify them. He pushed aside some spiny stalks.

Brody did the same in the next row over. "What exactly are we looking for?"

"The words antique. Or heirloom. That's with an *h*," he chided.

"Very funny," Brody fired back.

"We just need to find some blooming rose bushes that look like the ones we destroyed."

"I didn't get a good look at them in the first place."

"Just help me find something." Hutch was already exhausted by the hunt. Maybe he should have brought Valerie here to pick out what she wanted. No, he had already made her madder than a disturbed hornet by downing the tree and interrupting her morning routine.

And blocking her exit.

Crushing her landscaping.

Cracking the walkway.

When he thought about things that way, he understood her short fuse. Still, the woman was hot and cold. She was easy on the eyes, but hard in the head. She had a relaxed temperament when it came to getting a free lunch, but thin patience when it came to excuses. One minute, she spit fire. The next, she seemed to wrap Hutch's attention around her pinky finger with one look at her attractive figure.

"I said"—Brody slid his fingers between his lips and gave a high-pitched whistle—"stop your daydreaming. I think these over here might work."

"I'm coming."

Hutch high-stepped over a row of blooms as he followed Brody's pointed finger. "Bingo."

Just then, the nursery proprietor came out to join them, probably drawn by Brody's whistle more than the sound of his pickup truck's engine or their banter as they cluelessly perused what was available.

"Hello, boys," the widow woman called, her voice as hardened and sugary as the crystals in a jar of old honey. "You looking for something pretty for your lady friends?"

"Something like that, ma'am." Brody stifled a laugh.

"We found what we need."

"I've got some beautiful bougainvillea," the woman continued with a sales pitch regardless. "Plumbago that will bloom all summer. Aloe vera if you want something you don't have to worry with watering too much."

"We'll take six of these." Hutch picked up two of the large bushes by the rim of their black plastic pots and signaled for Brody to do the same. "How much?"

The woman named a price Hutch wasn't sure was enough to cover the cost of seeds, soil, and her labor. He wasn't about to take this woman for a ride.

"Are you sure?" He was prepared to pay much more.

"That's all I need," she insisted. "If you can pay with cash, I'd appreciate it."

Hutch nodded. "I can oblige with that." He and Brody loaded the plants, settling them into the back of the blue pickup. Hutch handed the woman a fifty-dollar bill, which was nearly double the price she quoted. "Keep the change," he insisted, not only glad to get a bargain but to make an old woman's day. Selling plants like this was part of her retirement livelihood, and the money would mean a great deal to her.

"Bless you, sweet boy." She beamed.

Had he been closer, he was sure she would have reached out to pinch his cheeks. Instead, he dipped his head, offered a final thanks, and headed back to the truck. He just hoped these plants would be to Valerie's liking—he wasn't ready to get into a princess-and-the-pea debate about whether or not these would suit her needs.

"Hey, Brody, I forgot to tell you," he called to Brody at

the tailgate. Hutch readied to enter the cab. "We also have to fix some cracks in her walkway."

"What?" Brody hinged the tailgate into place, locking it with a firm push. Then he dusted off his hands palm to palm. "All of this just because of a dog?"

Nod was still fresh on his mind, too, but he couldn't hang the entire chain of events on the neck of a sweet canine. "Actually," he corrected, "all of this for a woman."

"Some woman," Brody countered, but even though his words were in jest, Hutch chose to hear them as a compliment.

Because, even though he wouldn't admit it aloud, there was still something about Valerie that was getting to him. She was "some woman" all right, and even if nothing came of it, Hutch would correct the damage caused by the tree fall and try to do right by her.

A MIRROR REPLACEMENT in the bathroom was one line item on Penny's list. The goal was to make the space above the sink look more like a vanity. There was a mid-century rectangular medicine cabinet with beveled glass that, at one time, had probably been beautiful. But parts were splotchy, and the edges were worn and rusting. Although it did the job of reflection, it did little else in the space.

"Mirror, mirror, on the wall." Valerie squared her stance and spoke directly to it. "Who's the fairest choice of all . . . that will help me sell this house?" She held up a page from the shabby-chic book that offered several mirror style choices, and she tried to imagine which would look the best.

Each had ornate frames and were all rounded in shape. Whether oval or circular, they were affixed with a thick satin ribbon tie at the top and hung exactly at eye level flush against the wall.

They looked to her like the vanity option Penny had suggested.

Valerie had thought a small mirror would shrink the feel of the space, but the book insisted the opposite. That a thoughtfully placed, delicate mirror would enhance the beauty of a small space, making it appear more majestic than it was in reality.

She had to read those lines twice to make sure she understood the logic. Though, in truth, she was still skeptical.

She could order a piece like this online, but before she left the library, Quinn had directed her to a secondhand store that specialized in antiques, insisting, "I'm sure you'll find some things you can immediately use as well as some things a quick coat of paint might make work."

Quinn made it sound so easy.

And that was what Valerie had thought this project would be.

A little paint here. Some elbow grease there. A rug strategically placed. A new lamp to soften the light.

Not bathroom work. Not teardowns. And certainly not a whole new lexicon of design understanding.

She'd give the secondhand store a try. After all, she didn't have anything to lose.

With one decision made, she left the bathroom to return to the small living space. She lowered herself onto the edge of a petite settee, now considering this space in the full light of the afternoon. She closed the book and placed it at her side as she shut her eyes and took in a few deep breaths. This space was the center of activity during the two preteen summers she spent with Grandma Perry. During those stays, she passed through this room countless times during the day. But now, all she could remember were the evenings. She focused on capturing the tide of memories as they washed into her subconscious.

She saw the living space in her mind's eye as it once was. Every morning, her grandmother would push back the curtains to let the light in and wouldn't close them again until nightfall. Valerie knew because she remembered dark spilling into the space. The evening sky transformed outside this very window, and as it crept in, it brought with it the one aspect of rural Texas summers she loved the most.

Fireflies.

Valerie squeezed her eyes to hold on to the reformed memories. She could see fireflies lighting up the panes of glass like tiny flickering orbs begging for her attention.

And as the memory took shape, she could also hear her grandmother saying "yes" to her pleas. "Yes, child, go play with 'em for a while." Her grandmother's voice was soothing and safe. "Catch one in your hand. Hold on to its light."

Valerie remembered running out to the back lawn in her heart-patterned nightgown, the one she wore so often the cloth was nearly see-through from having gone through the wash so many times. But such devoted wear made it softer than anything else she owned, and the vibrant colors of each blush-colored heart somehow never lost their luster.

On those summer nights when she slipped outside, it never took long to catch a firefly by cupping her hands around one, then sliding her thumbs to the side to take a peek. The bug's bright light glowed against her skin. How Mother Nature managed to create such a creature was beyond her mind's comprehension then.

And even now.

She didn't understand the biological forces that made fireflies light up the way they did. But something about their mystery still held.

There were things in life just like that. Age didn't matter because the wonder remained.

Valerie opened her eyes and was back in the living room.

Alone.

But not lonely.

For the first time since she arrived, she could feel the presence of her grandmother wrapping around her like a warm blanket. A feeling of security overtook her, a hug from a loved one as if coming from beyond the grave.

The feeling was entirely new for Valerie. Never had she felt such a sensation, a tingling that seemed to come from an alignment of place and space that seized her without warning.

It wasn't uncomfortable. Just new.

And because of that, she wasn't sure what to do with the sensation.

For the time being, she simply let it come and then let it pass. Memories—and what they delivered in their wake—were tricky like that.

But if memories were all she had to deal with, she could

manage. Instead, she had much greater tasks before her, namely choices and decisions that would affect this place for years to come. She'd thought navigating those would be easy.

Yet the more time she spent under this roof, the more she realized they wouldn't be, because something tugged at her. She couldn't identify exactly what it was, but if the feelings persisted, she at least had time by herself to figure them out.

Now, the more pressing thing to figure out was how to implement shabby chic across the one-thousand-square-foot space that she was still exploring herself.

She shifted her position on the settee, which was one of only two lounging pieces left in the living room. The other was a wooden wingback chair. Both were in shades of gray upholstery. And, if Valerie was remembering correctly what Quinn had said, that hue was not in the palette family for shabby chic.

She turned to a color wheel at the back of the book.

"I'm right!" But that didn't mean she was at liberty simply to dump the pieces and replace them overnight with something that worked. Money spent here and money spent there would add up. So if there were a way to freshen the pieces without breaking the bank, she'd give it a try.

Thumbing through for additional ideas, she considered slip covers, accent pillows, and even painting the upholstery tacks in a complement shade to tie in with the rest of the room. The last option seemed to be the cheapest fix, and the idea of taking a small brush to dab, dab, dab sounded like fun. Besides, she had no use for the furniture anyway, so whatever was there would convey with the sale of the house.

If she could make the pieces attractive, she was sure to yield a higher purchase price.

Paging further, she got an idea for distressing wood furniture using vinegar. The chippy patina look was kind of interesting, and it certainly could add visual appeal to the generally bland table and two chairs that sat off the galley kitchen.

Before Valerie knew it, she had a laundry list of visual changes that were not only doable but looked enjoyable. She was a girl about to get her craft on!

With a loose plan in place, she texted her thanks to Quinn, who had shared her phone number before Valerie left the library. Quinn was incredibly friendly, but it was the right kind of friendly for Valerie. In fact, when Quinn pinged back with a happy face emoji and a link to the address of the secondhand store she had mentioned in person, Valerie was over the moon.

She checked the hours of the store before asking Quinn if she'd care to join her for some treasure hunting.

Quinn's second happy face emoji was followed by a time suggestion at the end of the day, which was perfect. That way, Valerie could scan the secondhand store for possibilities right away, have time the following day to take measurements if she needed, and she could always order online with rush shipping anything she absolutely couldn't find there or at Nailed It.

But a half hour before Valerie was going to head out, a triple knock at the door announced a visitor. The signature sound was this man's version of a bat signal.

"Bubba Hutchinson." She declared his arrival like a

voiceover actor by using his full name.

The surprise caught him off guard, for he snapped to attention and looked straight at her with deer-in-the-headlights eyes.

"Not what you were expecting?"

"You're who I was expecting," he corrected. He lowered his voice. "I just wasn't expecting you to call me that."

"It's your name," she said simply. She wasn't necessarily playing fair. Still, she couldn't resist the tease.

"A name not many people know," he reminded her. He brought a finger to his lips, making a slight *shhh* as if they were sharing a private piece of information.

Had they? Or was this some kind of ruse? Valerie didn't know, and she wasn't in a position to figure it out. She needed to finish a few cleaning projects before she left to meet Quinn. "What do you have for me, Bubba?"

Hutch lowered his finger, shaking his head as if to chastise her. But while his head communicated one thing, she swore the twinkle of his eyes communicated something entirely different.

He liked sparring.

Most men did.

Because when it came to their desire to one-up the opposite gender, they got more mileage out of the experience when they had to work a little harder.

And her ability to dish right back what Hutch was serving was a trait he probably wasn't used to in women.

But, then again, Valerie didn't think she was like most women around here. True, she was a city girl, but she could still hold her own in the country. She was no wallflower.

Though she did expect this guy to be bringing her flowers. At least the potted kind.

"I have some plants for you," he answered, pointing over his shoulder to where Brody stood at the edge of the blue pickup truck she recognized from the day before. He waved a hearty hello as she reciprocated with a tight-fingered acknowledgement of her own.

"Good." She was owed these, and it was still going to be work for her to tear out the old, replace it with the new, and get them watered so they would stay looking fresh. Landscaping, Penny had emphasized, did make a difference with buyers.

"Six should be just right for replacement."

Was it that many?

"But I'm not sure if these are what was there," Hutch admitted.

"Probably not." Antique roses were quite special, although she knew only the basics, not the specifics.

"But these are colorful. And they should be drought tolerant." He turned away to motion to Brody, who raised one of the plants by its container high in the air for her to see. Then, he started toward the spot where the bushes were going to be replaced.

"That first one looks really nice." Her eye noticed the blooms right away, and whatever it was sure looked a lot more healthy than the untended roses. "Are they all like that?"

"All the same. The row of them should look nice right there in the middle, especially to add some color. Shouldn't take long for us to get them in the ground."

"Wait. What?"

"Brody and me." He turned back toward her. "We'll do it right now, unless that presents some sort of major problem."

"I didn't know you were going to plant them."

"Nod's action, my fault," he said simply.

The words didn't make any sense to Valerie. Would it kill Hutch to remember not everyone was from Last Stand?

"Yesterday. The dog." He added the last two words louder, as if somehow they would make more sense that way.

They didn't. "I have no idea what you are talking about."

Hutch gave her a you've-got-to-be-kidding-me look.

But she didn't budge. "Nod?"

"He's the dog that ran under the tree." He eyed her as if trying to judge whether she really didn't know or she was just ribbing him. "Right when I was about to make the last cut, I saw him out of the corner of my eye, and I wasn't about to risk hitting him. The tree wasn't planned to fall on your driveway. But to save a dog, it's what I had to do."

To save a dog. The words rang in Valerie's ears.

"So yesterday you saved a dog?" Now it all started to add up. The haste. The surprise. And she'd thought it was simply a blundering mistake.

"Well, now that you're asking me, I'd say that Nod saved himself. Fast as a jackrabbit, that boy is."

But as much as Hutch might be downplaying the events, everything suddenly made sense to Valerie. Hutch didn't plan for the tree to fall on her driveway, not until Nod ran under it. That explained his shock when she swung open the door in her bathrobe ready to chew him out for his incompetence. He had even tried to use his sense of humor to appease her when she grew mad.

"I was rude to you yesterday," she whispered softly with a voice so meek she could barely hear her own words.

"No." Hutch took a step forward. "You didn't know—"

Before he could finish, Valerie's eyes brimmed with moisture. She was on the verge of a reaction she didn't want Hutch to see.

Chapter Eight

WHY WERE THE pretty ones always so complicated? Hutch closed his eyes and scrubbed his hand across his face, hoping that after his palm passed over his lids, he'd open them again to normalcy. He wanted to see a perfectly normal woman standing in a doorway with a perfectly normal look on her face.

Not one that looked like she was about to cry.

He opened first one eye and then the other.

Nope. He took in the sight of Valerie. *Still complicated.*

Hutch fought between the urge to comfort her and the urge to pull away so she could have personal space. Rather than doing either, he froze but settled for asking, "What's wrong?"

"I don't like the thought of killing animals."

"Neither do I. Which is why I didn't."

Valerie brought the tip of her index finger to the corner of her eye, dabbing as if she herself wasn't sure of what was happening. "Am I—"

"Crying?" They said the word together.

And as serious as the tears might have been, the chorus of their combined voice took them both by surprise. He couldn't help but draw in a breath that mirrored hers—and then let it out in a soft bit of laughter.

Laughter. Tears. Hutch still didn't quite know what was happening.

And if he didn't, Brody yards away surely didn't either. Behind him, Hutch could hear Brody's movements from truck to driveway with the plants. Since it didn't look like Hutch would be making his way there anytime soon, the process of moving them would at least keep his buddy busy in the short term.

"Let's talk about this." Hutch cut his hand through the space that separated him from Valerie. "And this." He moved his hand to the side of his face, stretching his index finger and miming a falling tear.

"I don't know why I'm so emotional all of a sudden."

Tenderly, he asked, "Did you have a dog recently pass away?"

"What?" Somehow what he intended as a heartfelt outreach had registered as nonsense. "No. I've never even owned a dog. Well," Valerie corrected herself, "not at my house."

"Okay." He didn't know what to make of that, but impromptu armchair psychiatry was all he had to work with here. "It's just that when I talked about Nod, you started to tear up."

"And then I was laughing," she added.

"Yes," he acknowledged, but the juxtaposition was still unclear to him. Women's codes were tough to crack.

Now it was Valerie's turn to scrub away the confusion. She brought both hands to her face, briefly buried herself, and came up for air only when she seemed to be in more control. "No tears," she announced, though he wasn't sure if she was giving herself an order or asking him a question.

So he simply repeated her words. "No tears."

"I didn't expect to go there. That's all."

"Go where?"

"My mind. That memory. I had totally forgotten it until . . ." Valerie's words disappeared into the air as quickly as her clarity of forming them.

So, she's clearly processing—something. Hutch knew the general look she wore. But he wasn't in a position to help her through whatever it was she was experiencing. "How about you go inside. Get some water. Sit down." He kept his voice as even as a hostage negotiator. "Brody and I are going to put these plants into the ground. Don't worry about a thing."

"Okay." She nodded. "I'm so sorry." All her sass and snark from the previous day was gone, replaced with a tenderness in her voice and a visual display of emotional vulnerability Hutch felt a strange urge to protect.

"There's nothing to be sorry about." When she backed up, he took a few reactionary steps forward, just in case she decided to pass out on top of everything else. A day before, he had offered a first aid kit to help with the cuts on her foot. Today, he was talking her into having a seat and taking a mental timeout from the complications of whatever was passing through her in that moment. "Do you want me to get you anything?"

"No."

"You sure?"

"I've got bottled water in the fridge. I'll get one of those."

"Good." Hydration in the middle of mental fog was good. "Take it easy. Relax. We're going to work, and I'll check on you right before we leave, if that's okay?"

She nodded.

"All right then." Hutch stepped back and closed the front door to give Valerie privacy. Nod had a way of pulling at the hearts of people in the neighborhood, but for a newcomer like Valerie, Hutch didn't think the pooch had that much clout.

There was something else going on with her. Hutch knew that much about women, but he didn't know enough to do any more than give her space in that moment. He just hoped that would be enough.

VALERIE FLICKED ON the faucet, leaned over the kitchen sink, and splashed cool water over her forehead and neck.

Was she completely losing her mind? Crying—over what? The mention of some neighborhood dog she didn't know. How was that even sensible?

She had been in Last Stand for two full days, and so far, her sanity scorecard was being sorely tested. The longer she was here, the less clearly she could think.

And Valerie previously never had a problem thinking clearly.

At work, she researched, made decisions after careful planning, and only took risks that were calculated. Upper management at the grocery store chain where she worked trusted her. Corporate decision-makers counted on her coolheaded, level thinking. So whether she was buying produce or securing contracts, she used data, reasoning, and common sense to make smart moves.

She didn't let people down.

She wasn't an emotional decision maker.

And she certainly wasn't a crier.

Yet she had teared up in front of someone during a time labeled a "vacation" from work.

This was completely unlike Valerie Perry.

She wanted to kick herself for wearing her feelings on her sleeve. That didn't happen in San Antonio, and that didn't need to happen here, especially with all the work she had to do in regard to the house.

Whatever emotional baggage was trying to surface, she needed to push it down so she could take care of the business at hand. That included reno and prep for a sale that needed to happen sooner rather than later.

Because now, she feared the longer she stayed here readying for a major real estate transaction, the more brittle she would become from swirls of stress and sentimental recollections she didn't even realize had been weighing on her.

She raised her head and cut the stream of water running from the faucet. She grabbed a nearby tea towel, one of several left behind she had been using earlier to dry dishes. She had dirtied a cup and saucer for coffee at breakfast and a plate for her grilled cheese sandwich and veggie chips lunch. Since there was no dishwasher, she was cleaning, drying, and replacing as she went through each meal with dishes.

Orderly.

Methodical.

See, you can do this. This was the pace she needed to focus on.

She folded the towel neatly on the counter before opening the fridge, grabbing a bottle of water from the case she had brought with her, and unscrewing the top with a force that served as an outlet for her personal frustration of nearly losing it in front of another person.

A near stranger, no less.

At least, he started out as a stranger. Now she didn't know what to call the man she knew as Bubba Hutchinson. She had seen him several times, both at this home and at his own place of business. She had shown him her early morning self, her I-need-bandages self, her vegetarian self, and even a more carefree, joking self. They'd jabbed, they'd bantered. She had raised her voice. She laughed. She learned more about him, and he, in turn, her.

What was this?

She tilted back her head and took another long drink of water. When she swallowed, she leveled her gaze at nothing in particular and placed the side of the bottle against her neck, the cool plastic refreshing her skin that burned hot with confusion.

If she made another trip to the library, she might just have to peruse their self-help offerings. She didn't dare type in her litany of worry into an internet search for fear of what craziness might appear.

She'd call her parents tonight. A quick talk with her father in particular might yield some insight into why she was feeling so on edge. Did he experience a level of decision-making anxiety when he was cleaning out the house? Did the home trigger any memories for him that he hadn't previously known? The questions were already stirring inside of her, but

Valerie would have to keep a lid on them until much later in the evening.

For the time being, she had to keep an eye on Hutch. Because something told her if she didn't, she might just end up with another major surprise outside her driveway, on the walkway, or some other place for which she hadn't bargained. She didn't need any more derailments.

When she finished the water and peeked out a window, Hutch and Brody were bent over the side of her driveway, their bodies half obscured by her Kia. But what she was able to see was a burst of color that now divided her property more definitively from Mrs. Lydia Lang's. Where antique roses once bloomed now stood several leafier plants in a vibrant green with bright fuchsia blooms that popped in contrast. They looked welcoming and fresh, providing quite a visual show for anyone who parked in the driveway.

Plenty of roses still stood in quiet beauty along the rest of the driveway, but the fresh additions added new life to that side of the yard. Penny was right; plants made a difference.

Valerie stepped back from the window and went into the bathroom before grabbing a ball cap from the bedroom. She pushed her hair off her neck into a makeshift ponytail that she pulled through the hole in the back of the cap. Adjusting the cap into place, she was already feeling better after having a bit of time to herself and getting some hydration back.

Maybe the hard work and chemical fumes of the day were getting to her. Actually, considering all she had done— scrubbing the tub with a compound cleaner, using ammonia on the floors, spraying down the sinks with disinfectant spray—the unhealthy mixture of fumes had probably affected her.

That was it.

Seeing the flowers up close, getting a bit of fresh air, and going to meet Quinn for an indoor treasure hunt was sure to make her feel much better.

And if she needed, she'd still make that phone call to her parents, if for no other reason than to check-in with a conversation rather than just exchange texts like she had been doing with them both since her arrival on Sunday evening.

Valerie grabbed her purse and keys, swung open the front door, and locked the entrance behind her. Stepping into the sun, she pulled the brim of the cap down ever so slightly to shield her eyes.

"Hey there," Hutch called. "We're just finishing up."

"I see that," she said.

Brody was patting an area at the far end of the driveway around her mailbox. In what was once just a grassy spot that surrounded a white wooden pole, there were now two knee-high plants on either side. They weren't like the blooming ones Hutch was finishing.

She pointed toward the mailbox. "Where'd those come from?"

"Same place as these." Hutch stood and opened his arms wide in presentation over the beautifully planted additions. "Those two were bonuses from the master gardener who sold us these. We got a steal," he insisted.

Valerie looked from Hutch to Brody and back again. "But nothing was damaged over there." *Or was it?*

"Consider them freebies. They should be good for full sun. Minimal care. Do you like the way they frame the mailbox?"

They probably should have consulted her first, but the new plants did add that all-important curb appeal, and in a prime location. She could forgive their oversight. "They look great."

"I thought so too." He flashed a thumbs-up at Brody, who reciprocated before walking the shovel he was using back to the pickup.

"You didn't have to do that."

"I know," Hutch insisted. "But I needed to do this." He nodded toward the plants where he stood, his shirt pushed back to expose ample forearms bronzed from the sun. Tiny rivulets of sweat rolled down over muscles she had no idea he had. "And I still need to do that." He tilted his head toward the walkway. "But, before I do anything, how are you feeling?"

"Much better." That was the truth. "I don't know what came over me." That, also, was the truth.

"Don't worry about it." He waved a dismissive hand.

Valerie wanted to do just that. "In fact, I've got an errand to run."

"Then don't let us keep you." The pickup truck was parked on the street, and they both followed the line of sight down the driveway. "You'll have room to back out just fine."

"Are you going to fix the walkway now?" Granted, she wasn't sure what level of work that project involved, but it still seemed like a major undertaking to begin so late in the afternoon.

"We can at least get started. Brody's going to help me with supplies, but then he's got electrical jobs tomorrow.

He's working on an apprenticeship."

Valerie nodded. She couldn't, after all, assume total commitment of time and resources from them both, especially when all of this was unexpected. The guilt over monopolizing so much of their time—for a mistake she now understood wasn't their personal blunder but the result of a random decision by a neighborhood dog—tugged at her. "Look, don't worry about the walkway. Really, you two have done enough, and the additions look even better than what was here before."

"But the cracks—"

"Are not your problem." Valerie was changing her tune. "Those are mine to deal with."

"You know how to replace flagstone?" He lowered the side of one eyebrow in such a way that reminded her of James Franco.

And, for the record, James Franco had the sexiest eyebrows of any actor on the planet as far as she was concerned.

But back to walkway repair.

She didn't know the first thing about it.

But she wasn't about to say so. "I'll manage."

Hutch shook his head. "No way. Besides, Penny called, and when Penny wants something—"

"I nearly forgot about that." So much was happening in such a short time. "You're right."

Hutch seized the words. "So then, it's settled. I'm helping. You won't get rid of me until this job is done." He placed one hand in his pocket and smiled a Cheshire cat grin of satisfaction.

If their earlier encounter had been light and their exchange more playful, she might have hugged him out of sheer thankfulness and joy. But with her emotional unsteadiness, she didn't want to alarm Hutch—or make herself teeter—with contact or any physical display.

Still, it took every ounce of restraint to keep her from throwing her arms around the broad shoulders of a man who was offering free help, especially one who looked as ruggedly handsome doing manual labor as he did. She hadn't noticed it the previous morning, but something about the late afternoon sun's rays lighting his brown hair with golden highlights and the V-shape of skin peering at her from the unbuttoned top of his shirt collided in a sexy combination she didn't know would excite her.

But, oh, did it!

Chapter Nine

"I JUST DON'T know." Valerie glanced at Quinn to see what she thought.

"Shabby chic isn't about pieces in isolation," Quinn insisted. "It's about the combination." She pointed to the two throw pillows Valerie was considering. One was a frilly and fun collection of quilted lace. The other was a square pillow with a screen-printed picture of a crow wearing a string of pearls.

"I've never seen anything like this." Valerie couldn't help but laugh at the whimsical design. It looked like the bird was flying over Paris or some other large European city.

"Which is precisely why it works as a statement piece."

"Some statement." Valerie shifted her weight to one heel. "And, just to be clear"—she pointed from one pillow to the next—"what, exactly, does this combo say?"

Quinn leaned forward and fluffed each pillow one by one. She raised the white lace one, moving it as if it were talking. "This says, I'm exactly what you need to make the sitting area welcoming."

"And that?" Valerie pointed to the crow one, trying not to laugh too loudly. She still wasn't sure if the image was supposed to be humorous, satirical, or something else entirely. Whatever the case, she couldn't deny that an image like that would be a conversation starter for anyone who walked into the home.

"This says"—Quinn raised the bird pillow—"buy this house or else."

"Well then, I definitely need that one," Valerie decided.

"Actually, you need both." Quinn pushed them in her direction, and Valerie accepted them into her embrace. "Because all pillows are buy-one-get-one-free."

"True." Valerie tilted her head to tell the crow, "So I guess you're coming home with me."

Quinn clapped in happy satisfaction.

"You are enjoying this far too much," Valerie said, though, in truth, she was thankful for the company. Having someone to shop with and share laughs gave her a chance to relax. It felt like she and Quinn had been friends for much longer than four hours.

"I am starved for playtime around here. Ever since I took the job, all I seem to do is work. Or think about work." Quinn added after a brief pause, "Or work on work."

Valerie could relate. "Before I became a buyer, I kept trying to prove myself. Never turning down a project, putting in later hours than everyone else, trying to set myself apart."

"So it paid off?"

"It did." She had the job of her dreams in a city she loved. "And how about for you?"

"Well . . ." Quinn traced her finger along the top of a wooden bureau as they continued to browse the secondhand store. "I wanted to study librarianship, I earned my master's degree, and I was able to come back to my hometown to be a librarian when lots of people in my graduating class are still out looking for full-time jobs with benefits. So . . ." She made a show of miming in the air. "Check."

"Congratulations. That's really impressive." Valerie meant it.

"Thanks." Quinn lifted her hand and paused. "It's still a bit strange, though, to be back here and run into people I used to know. Or my parents know. Don't get me wrong," she cut into her own litany of thoughts. "It's wonderful to do the work I do in Last Stand. But it's not exactly ripe for my social life."

Valerie followed what Quinn meant. "Aaah, there's the rub."

"Shakespeare!" Quinn raised her finger in the air as if she were a detective who had just figured out a clue. "That's a line from *Hamlet*."

Valerie furrowed her brow. "Is it? Must be one of those sayings stuck in the recesses of my mind from my own college days."

Quinn looked pleased as punch. "Well, cheers to whichever professor helped it get stuck there."

"Back to your personal life." Talking about Quinn's was a welcome distraction for Valerie's nonexistent dating status as of late. She had experienced a dry spell. Or, at least, that was what she was telling herself, even though she wanted to eventually find the perfect guy and work toward something long-term.

The two continued to stroll through the store, Valerie holding on to the pillows. "Is that hard to have here? I mean, meeting men. Making connections. Is it hard to date in Last Stand?"

"For me it is." There was a quiet resignation in Quinn's voice. Not library quiet. More like sad quiet. "Either guys who come into the library are too old for my tastes, not datable because they're already in committed relationships, or—"

"Ouch!" Valerie sensed there was a bigger story there, but she didn't ask.

"Or they're just not that interesting."

"So they're not into Shakespeare?"

"They don't have to be into Shakespeare." Quinn shrugged. "They just have to be into something. Have a passion for doing whatever it is they do. Be someone unique. Unpredictable in the good kind of ways."

Valerie had never taken the time to make an actual list, but Quinn's criteria were what she valued in a guy as well.

Except maybe for the unpredictable part.

Valerie liked predictable. Orderly. Organized.

Yet that didn't always translate in the dating pool.

"Do you think there's a difference between being spontaneous and being unpredictable?"

Quinn brought a finger to her chin. "I think so."

Like Hutch. The guy had a monopoly on keeping things unpredictable.

"To me, being unpredictable isn't a bad thing."

Maybe Valerie had been too quick to judge men in the past. There was a fine line to walk when it came to too much or too little of any characteristic. But had her prior expectations with men been too harsh? Did she need to reconsider priorities?

It was refreshing to have a sounding board at least.

"Ready for some good news?"

Valerie was always ready for that. "Tell me."

"You're young." Quinn pointed a thumb at Valerie, then turned it toward herself. "I'm young." She pressed her finger against the fabric of her shirt. "We'll find our princes."

"Let's hope."

She flashed an assured smile. "I know what we can do in the meantime." Her eyes gleamed wide.

"What's that?"

"Shop till we drop!" Her facial expression lit like a kid at Christmas.

Valerie couldn't help but laugh at that. "I'm in."

"What else do you need?"

"A bathroom mirror, for sure. A lamp for the living room." Valerie had a laundry list in her mind. "Maybe a small chest of drawers to replace the monster of the one in the bedroom. I want to make every room look bigger than it is and feel welcoming enough that the first buyer who walks in opens a wallet and says, 'Sold!'"

"That's how that works." Quinn played along, her comeback laced with a bit of sarcasm.

"I hope so."

"Well, in that case, we need to get after it." Quinn picked up the pace.

They found a mirror, a gorgeous white candelabra, a vintage light fixture with hanging cut glass that could be used to jazz up the simple overhead one in the kitchen, and two matching lamps with soft ballet-pink shades and patina bases that looked so pretty Valerie had to buy them both.

On the way out the shop, a small collection of brass pencil sharpeners caught her eye. Each was a quirky design, something perhaps lovingly collected at one time that was now turned over to this used shop to be bought and sold in separation. There was a bit of sadness to that idea, but she could also imagine the reciprocal joy in new buyers finding something unexpectedly fun to take home as a treasure.

She sidestepped to get a closer look at the two dozen or so pieces, and one immediately caught her eye. "How much?" She pointed to the one she wanted and asked the proprietor.

The owner held up one hand with all five fingers outspread. Five dollars was what she'd pay for a latte at the shop near her apartment complex in San Antonio, so choosing to use the money for this treasure instead was a no-brainer.

Besides, the tiny antique wasn't for her. She had someone very particular in mind who would be the perfect match for this special piece.

WHEN VALERIE ARRIVED back to the bungalow, she half expected to see Hutch's blue pickup still parked on the street. When it wasn't, her heart sank.

Perhaps the regularity of seeing Hutch in her yard, at her doorstep, at the restaurant, and back again was the reason for her slight disappointment at his absence.

At least, that was what she told herself.

She pulled into the driveway, stepped out of her car, and was accosted by the smell of fragrant blooms. The roses mingling with the scent of the new additions created a harmony of smells that instantly lifted her mood.

A beautiful way to arrive home. She deemed Hutch's work and his choice of selection absolutely perfect.

On the walkway that wound from the neighbor's side of the driveway, there was a work-in-progress underway. Luckily, the movement of flagstones and addition of new gravel wasn't an eyesore. The low-to-the-ground changes simply looked like replacements were ongoing, which was pretty much how the rest of the bungalow was inside anyway.

Penny would be by later in the week for final pictures, so Valerie certainly had her work cut out for her in trying to get the most photo-worthy areas cleaned, staged, and ready.

She reached into the back seat to grab her secondhand store treasures. She'd retrieve the lamps she placed in the trunk later.

Balancing her new purchases, she made her way to the front door. There, a small note was secured by Scotch tape at eye level. It was folded once so no one could see inside, and its edges lifted on the occasional breeze. Valerie unfolded it with one hand and read the simple words from Hutch.

See you tomorrow afternoon.

He signed his name with five letters surrounded by a quick sketch of flames lapping around them.

Of course. What else should she expect from a barbeque brother?

The sight of hand-drawn fire made Valerie smile and, oddly, a little warm on the inside. Even on paper, Hutch was unpredictable. The note was cute.

But what was added to the bottom wasn't as easy to discern.

The digits of his phone number stared back at her. And while she thought perhaps it was a simple calling card approach in case she had any questions about the walkway, she also thought it might be more.

Because below the number were two lines.

Call me.

Looking forward to chatting when you do.

Chatting? Did that mean something other than for reasons that brought them together in the first place?

Valerie flipped the note over in case there was more. Did tree trimmers who performed handyman work "chat" with their clients—especially their nonpaying ones? And did Hutch always "look forward" to future interactions, or was that a line directed specifically at her?

This is unpredictable.

She rolled her shoulders and fished for her keys in her purse, stashing the note there. Perhaps she was reading far too much into an innocent piece of scribbled correspondence. There was no reason to project hope for future communication for reasons even she didn't quite understand.

She was having a hard time making sense of much today. Besides, there was no reason to blow anything out of proportion.

Although she was single and found Hutch attractive, there was no future to consider. He lived in Last Stand. She lived in San Antonio. He was as country as they came. She was a city girl through and through. He was a red-blooded meat lover. She was a vegetarian. They couldn't possibly have enough in common to sustain anything more than a temporary friendship during what was borrowed time for her anyway.

Her life was not here because the things she loved the most didn't exist in Last Stand. She enjoyed the bustle of city streets and the rhythm of her work week. She had carved a life, and perhaps even one day that would turn into roots through a husband, a family, and a future in San Antonio. Now that she had found a place that fit her, she wanted to stay in it.

And once she sold this house, she could return to that life.

All she had here were faded, fuzzy memories. Coming here didn't feel like home. The sensation of being in the bungalow was more like a hotel experience, as if she were simply a visitor.

The home really was beautiful, but Valerie didn't need it. She couldn't afford to keep it. Besides, it was bound to make some buyer incredibly happy.

She tried to keep her thoughts on the house, yet as she went through the motions of her evening and nighttime routines, her mind slid to thoughts of Bubba Hutchinson. She didn't call him. A chat over the phone was too committal, especially when she would see him the next day. Yet he fired her up in all kinds of different ways and drew emotions from her she wasn't prepared to feel.

She had energy she never expected after just reading that simple note from him. Something about it made all parts of her body hyperaware, heightening her senses even as she paced through a nighttime routine that should have wound her down. Instead, thoughts of Hutch ratcheted the intensity up a notch.

How could a man she barely knew do that? And, more importantly, what did it mean to her carefully constructed life that he was able to do so?

Chapter Ten

"I NEED TO talk to you boys." Wanda Hutchinson had a tone that every mother seemed to possess in her arsenal of attention-getting tools. Hers was a low tenor, and she meant business.

Hutch could see the message written all over her face.

"Be right there." He balled his apron and tossed it into a kitchen hamper that held an assortment of stained sauce cloths, grease rags, and barbeque smoke-laden fabrics. Several times a week, his mother took home the soiled items, ran them through the wash, and brought them back. Fresh aprons and clean rags were a part of the business Hutch had previously taken for granted.

But as he readied to take over the reins, he noticed everything.

"Have a seat here." Wanda pointed to a small square table in the kitchen area beneath an AC vent, a workspace that doubled as a break room space for whoever needed it. Today, it was going to serve as a conference table. Wanda and Todd Hutchinson sat opposite each other, which left the next generation of Hutchinsons to fill in the space on each side of them. Hutch took his seat right as Cole did.

Informal meetings weren't unusual, especially to deal with a special event, big order, or upcoming catering job at

The Hut. But what was unusual was that none of those jobs were on the docket, at least not this week.

Judging by his father's posture and his mother's stern countenance, this was a formal meeting. Hutch took his seat and sat ramrod straight.

"What's going on?" He looked from his mother to his father to Cole and back again.

"Your father and I want to talk to you."

Todd Hutchinson leveled a stern look. "What you boys are doing is not working."

"What are you talking about?" Hutch leaned forward.

"This." Wanda pointed from Cole to Hutch and back again. "You two are bickering as if you are still children."

"I'm confused." Hutch had said little to Cole all day.

Wanda shook her head. "I'm not talking about just today."

"Day in, day out," his father underscored.

Hutch's chin dipped toward his chest. *Guilty.*

Wanda had much more to say. "You want one thing"— she held out an upturned open hand to Hutch—"and you want another." She mirrored the movement with her other hand toward Cole. She moved each arm up and down like a human balance scale. "And all that's happening is an idea over here and an idea over there. No steadiness. No compromise."

Hutch had an idea of what prompted this. "Did Cole come to you?"

"He didn't have to come to me."

"We've been seeing it play out for months," his father added.

"Is this about the future of The Hut?" Hutch knew as much, but he wanted to lay it all out on the table for clarity's sake.

His father sighed. "It's always about the future of The Hut."

"We watch you two boys. We always have," his mother said. "And we've been seeing things that concern us."

"Such as?" Hutch was doing all the prompting; Cole was noticeably silent. Maybe this wasn't a conversation purely driven by his parents.

Cole played a part in this.

Son of a biscuit. Hutch should have seen this coming. Cole had always been a whiny tattletale.

"What did he tell you?" Hutch demanded to know.

"Now don't raise your voice," his mother warned.

"You'll know when I raise my voice."

"Nobody's raising their voices." His father brokered the tension. "Cole just has some ideas here." He turned toward him. "And we need to hear him out."

"That's what this is about." Hutch blew out a breath before crossing his arms over his chest, his posture less rigid now as he settled into his chair.

"Yes." Cole closed the space Hutch made by backing away from the confrontation. "You haven't listened to any of my ideas—"

"I've listened," Hutch countered. "In fact, that's all I've done. Every time you have a new idea about corn casserole or asparagus or—"

"Who said anything about asparagus?"

"Asparagus, artichoke, whatever it was." Hutch was concerned with the big picture. "Bottom line is, you were gassing about menu updates and went behind my back to make a change I never authorized. None of this makes any sense for our customers."

"Which just goes to prove my point." Cole's face held a smug look Hutch knew well from their years of growing up together. "You don't listen. Because when it comes to what our customers want, you really have no idea."

Stiffness settled into Hutch's jaw and neck. A personal attack to his knowledge of what he had spent over a decade of his life doing was quite a wallop. He had been working at The Hut since he was fourteen, toddling around in it for long before that. He was following in the footsteps of what his father had done and his father before him.

Barbeque was in his blood.

And to imply Hutch understood little when he had mastered so much was a low blow.

But leave it to Cole to hit below the belt. Where it hurt. Again.

"Our customer base is different now than they were."

"Says who?"

"I do." Wanda's voice resurfaced, her simple words so firm and direct they demanded both the brothers' attention. "Listen to me." But as she proceeded, her upper body pivoted slightly toward Hutch; the words were directed at him, even though she tried to look equally to Cole. "You can't rest on laurels and traditions. Not in this business."

Hutch wanted to cut in with a *why not*, but he bit his lip to keep from interrupting. His mother might be turning over the reins of the business, but she was the matriarch of the family. Hutch, frustrated as he could get sometimes, was still not one to outright disrespect her. Besides, he needed to prove his earlier point that he was a good listener.

So he bent his ear toward his mother as she continued. "We're not 100 percent sure what this place needs. Your father and I thought we did, but our way of thinking is as dated as these walls." She paused as if considering her next line carefully. "We want you to see projections for this quarter and end of year. You need to be looking at these things more than you both are."

His father inhaled deeply, holding his breath a split second as if for strength before letting it go. "You need to see what we see."

Hutch was now scared to ask, but luckily Cole did. "And what exactly do you see?" So, he and his brother were actually in the same boat. Whatever bombshell financial secrets his parents were getting ready to unload, Cole was clueless.

"It's not good." His father's words dripped slowly, his shoulders dropping. He wore the look of a man crushed by more than a daily grind and typical entrepreneurial stresses.

"We want you boys to look over these figures." Wanda slid manila envelopes that had been poised next to her on the table to each brother. "See what we see," she warned, "and then find a way out of it."

Hutch's entire throat soured as he struggled to swallow the lump that had formed. He reached for the envelope, though accepting its contents felt like defeat.

COLE HAD AMBUSHED him.

But now, just minutes later, when Hutch was alone, the whole incident seemed like a drop in the bucket compared to bigger ownership problems.

Hutch sought refuge in the cab of his pickup. He spread the contents of the envelope next to him, reading every word and double-checking the sales figures he saw.

Projections didn't look good. Spring was their peak time, and they were in the thick of that season. Yet sales to date for this fiscal year were less than they had been for each of the five years prior.

Hutch gulped hard.

If sales were dim now, they would be dead on arrival by year's end.

Something had to give.

But additions to the menu couldn't be the answer. At least not the only answer.

Hutch turned over hypotheses in his head. He tried to find one thing among the ideas tumbling like laundry that he could lay his finger on to say simply, "*There. That's what needs to be fixed.*"

Pushing the menu aside, Hutch considered all the moving parts of the business. He knew about increases in freight costs and property taxes. But what else was contributing to the squeeze?

The cost of food and supplies? Those had risen, but not sharply in the past year. They could manage beef and pork fluctuations at market price. There was nothing there to trim.

Labor? He wasn't about to suggest a cutback on any employees. Their work force was local and valuable. They relied on everyone they employed.

Occupancy costs? The building was paid for, but perhaps it did need some cosmetic freshening. Maybe customers were noticing certain things and making choices based on that.

But even as Hutch privately admitted some renovation would be nice, he wasn't entirely convinced. Sure, someone might turn their nose up at the walls or make a snide comment about the small restrooms, but ultimately no one came to The Hut for the décor or a potty stop. They came for food.

And they made barbeque better than anyone.

But does everyone know that?

A question of reach was one he couldn't answer. Old-timers and long-time locals knew about The Hut, but what about people who were new to the area?

People like Valerie.

Rather inconveniently, he couldn't shut off attraction to her even when business decisions should have monopoly on his thoughts.

But Hutch's life never involved just one set of responsibilities. Even today, he still needed to head to Valerie's since he had promised to complete repairs on the walkway. Hutch was loyal—almost to a fault—because when he said he'd do something, he did it.

Even if that meant shifting his time from thinking about the future to help someone in the present.

And even if he was dog tired after putting in a full day's work already.

He restacked the papers before sliding them back into

the manila envelope. Then, he turned the key in the ignition and drove to Valerie's. This vegetarian who had unexpectedly flew onto his radar was some city girl from San Antonio with a fancy job that probably came with retirement benefits and actual business cards. Would she have come to The Hut on her own accord? Would she have taken a risk on a local place if Brody had not mentioned it that first morning she stood at the door in her bathrobe?

No, she would not have stepped foot in their barbeque market. She wouldn't have known about it, and it wasn't her usual fare.

But once she did, she enjoyed it. Hutch smiled at the memory of her face, alight with pleasure. She had enjoyed fresh food and warm side dishes. Including Cole's ridiculous casserole addition.

Hutch never liked crediting his younger brother, but Cole might be partially right. The menu needed to continually attract customers. But the way he had gone about the change was all wrong. Customers didn't need to be surprised. They just needed to be made aware.

That meant educating a whole new generation of restaurant goers—vegetarians included.

"Advertising." Hutch spoke the single word aloud, saying it like a bingo card win. "Advertising!" He spoke the word louder, more enthusiastically, connecting the dots. Knowledge might well be the answer to attracting more customers.

Did The Hut advertise? Rarely. They sponsored a few junior league sports teams, ran an ad in the local newspaper now and again, but really just relied on word of mouth. They

AUDREY WICK

didn't even have a billboard or interstate sign presence to direct people to where they were located in Last Stand.

But if those things hadn't been needed in the past, why try it now? Hutch pressed his foot against the gas pedal.

As his MPH gauge revved, so did his mind. He knew the answers.

Because my generation is digital.

We're tech savvy.

And our worlds are controlled by the devices we carry with us.

Hutch needed to meet customers where they were so their choices in dining could be available to them as well.

Advertising was key, but not in traditional ways. That was what he had been missing.

When had he even looked at ratings on dining apps and online review sites? He had been unengaged with social media for so long he wasn't even sure how much people shared regarding The Hut.

Or if they shared only positive comments and experiences.

Had negative press been swirling?

He wanted to turn around, head home, and take a digital dive in order to see what he could uncover. The answers to at least some of their worries had to be related to what others were saying, sharing, and spreading. And if he could be an active player in that game instead of a sidelined unobserver, he might be able to make tracks.

Positive ones.

Profitable ones.

Ones of which he, and his parents, could be proud. Taking a chance like this was worth a shot.

Still, before he threw himself into a world of digital research and marketing, there was a more immediate matter at hand, one that didn't involve his brain too heavily.

Just his brawn.

And as he closed the distance between his day job and what was becoming a slightly personal one, he was more than ready to show off his muscles to a woman who, though she was a fish out of water in Last Stand, was a catch Hutch couldn't seem to shake from his line.

What was it about Valerie Perry that drew her to him in ways he couldn't understand? The more he was around her, the more he saw the warmth beneath the wit. Stripping away her sass, Valerie was open in a manner that allowed him to be completely honest with her.

He had even told her his real name. On the first day he met her.

He still shook his head at the forwardness of that. Why he let his guard down and poured out something so private remained a mystery to him. Yet he wasn't one to second-guess his choices. He had shared something intimate with her, and she replied in kind. He didn't feel stripped or humiliated. He felt . . .

Understood.

Chapter Eleven

VALERIE PUSHED THE living room furniture into the center of the room, leaving only the wood stove exposed. Not only could she now see what she truly had and make important decisions about what to keep and what had to go, but she could also get to the walls.

Oh, the walls!

In the library book she was using as her guide, there was a beautiful combination of whitewashed wainscoting at chair-rail height matched with pastel walls painted above. The combination was like reverse daybreak, cozy yet inviting. Earlier that day, she had brought along the book to Nailed It to match a paint sample to the shade she saw. She had left with semi-gloss paint, primer, and all the tools she needed to make this project happen.

Each step forward was progress. And as long as Valerie kept heading that direction, she'd make her way to the end goal.

With access cleared and the walls readied, she took a flathead screwdriver, pried it beneath the paint lid in several locations, and waited for the audible *poof* to indicate when to lift the lid. The color saturated the top of the can in a sheen so perfect, she wanted to poke it with her finger just to make sure the hue was real.

Yet she resisted the temptation since, she suspected, she'd have paint in places she couldn't control soon enough.

With her hair tied back, her work clothes in place, and her enthusiasm for the task at hand, Valerie grabbed the complementary stirring stick with the authority of a symphony conductor. She eased the stick into the paint can, the flat ruler shape cutting through the paint to mix any last bits that hadn't released during the mixing process.

Taking her time, following protocol, and advancing with care were the ways forward in this DIY process.

And once she got her hands on the roller, there was no turning back.

A meditative ease pervaded the process of dipping, rolling, and coating. The paint applied to the wall magnetically, as if every little molecule was as excited to be there as Valerie was to put it there. The method itself was soothing, a repetitive and fulsome process in which she could be completely self-absorbed yet not feel the slightest pang of guilt for doing so.

Valerie floated through the process on a high of more than paint fumes. As she transformed the space, something bloomed in her as well. Her previous anxiety melted away as she rolled and rolled, her body enjoying the monotony as much as her mind. Valerie was feeling fine.

And, in no time at all, the place was looking that way too. Or, at least, it was headed in that direction. Truly, this pastel had been the right choice. It was neutral without being bland, soft without being overly feminine. Against the wainscoting, it provided a subtle pop of contrast that would soon become a fabulous backdrop for her shabby-chic décor and furniture staging. She could hardly wait to see it all come together.

As she worked, thoughts slid to her grandmother. Had she liked the original eggshell walls? This home? Or at some point had it, too, become a burden to her?

Perhaps not, if she had chosen to live her last years here, surrounded by her things.

In an act of love, Val Perry had passed her greatest asset to Valerie. Now, Valerie's final act of love in remembrance of her grandmother—regardless of the shifting and sometimes incomplete memories she had of her—would be to make this legacy gift something that could shine brightly and provide years of life to someone new.

Duty bound, Valerie stretched high, bent low, eased one way, and lunged the other to cover four walls of the living room, the small space of the front entrance, the side wall of the kitchen and the space below its cabinets with paint that would give the home a new skin.

Taking a break to grab some water, she checked her phone for messages. She hadn't heard an earlier alert for voicemail, but now her phone signaled she had one. She was so in the DIY zone it was hard to pry herself from the fervor of it all.

She cupped the phone to her ear, listening to a message from her newest friend. Quinn had called to let her know she found more design books that she added digitally to Valerie's library card. She said she would drop them by after work.

Front door service?

"That's thoughtful," Valerie mouthed as she finished Quinn's message. She squeezed the phone in gratitude as she lowered it from her ear. *People here are so nice.*

Valerie returned the phone to the counter and took another long drink of water. Between her communication with Quinn, conversations with Hutch, and even her dealings with Brody, she had met more new people in just a few days' time in Last Stand than she had in a month back in San Antonio. Sure, she waved to neighbors, made occasional small talk on the elevator, exchanged pleasantries with the building staff, had friends she met for coffee or a quick bite to eat at a River Walk café . . . but something about this place was different.

Was it the rural atmosphere, or did it have more to do with the bungalow itself? Situated squarely in a residential neighborhood, she couldn't escape others, especially when the home had needs that involved help from people at the hardware store, the library, and even random tree-trimmers-turned-lunch-conversationalists like Bubba Hutchinson.

Hutch. Valerie placed the water bottle on the kitchen counter. *Bubba.* He was a quite a character.

And, like clockwork, just as the thought of him crossed her mind, there was a knock at the front entrance.

When Valerie swung open the door, it was Hutch, following through with his word.

"As promised, here I am." He presented himself like a trophy.

"So you are." Valerie added without considering how it might sound to him, "I was just thinking about you."

As soon as the words escaped her mouth, she realized her mistake. The punch-drunk look of a lovesick teenager washed over Bubba Hutchinson's face. "You were?" He heard something she hadn't intended.

"Yes." *No.* She was as mixed up as a Rubik's Cube.

Yet Valerie had no time to solve the puzzle because Hutch made a bold move. He took a step toward her, encircled his hand around her waist, and repeated with something close to stars in his eyes, "I've been thinking about you too."

TOO CLOSE, TOO close. Alarm bells were sounding all throughout Valerie's head as Hutch was being unpredictable.

Again.

The brashness of his movements was a complete shock, paralyzing her voice as well as her body. Hutch's arms were around her in a surprise embrace, and her muscles didn't know if they should tense, relax . . .

Or completely turn to putty.

She could sidestep him with ease. She could tell him to move back. Nonverbally, his lower abdomen was directly in range for a swift punch had she wanted to give him a piece of her initial reaction.

But being close to Hutch solicited a whole new reaction. She tuned in to everything about him, her senses heightened to aspects of him she hadn't previously allowed herself to notice.

His scent was luring, a heady mixture of nature and hard work that summoned her closer. The soft cotton of his shirt skimmed her own, the sensation wildly and surprisingly evocative. His skin, balmy from the heat, radiated a warmth that drew her in, calling her to stay in his embrace.

Her pulse quickened, her heart raced, and she couldn't think straight. Was it Hutch? His nearness?

Or was her body preparing for a response that even her mind didn't yet know?

Hutch was dynamic and direct. He had an ease about him that made his personality unexpectedly charming, if not a bit rough around the edges. Manual labor had toned his body in natural, striking ways. He was like a cover model for rural, rugged attractiveness.

He was different than men she knew, different from those she had previously dated. He wasn't mired in pretenses. He didn't hide behind a staunch professional wardrobe. No three-piece suits or designer duds for Bubba Hutchinson.

He didn't need them.

His austerity refused to be finely dressed in constricting deceits. On the contrary, the clothes matched the man. Even in the short time Valerie had known him, what she saw was who he was.

And that bit of authenticity was refreshing.

Hutch held her in such a way that forced her to think quickly, yet he wasn't boxing her in to prevent her from making a move.

Whether he knew he was giving her such control or not, the sense of personal empowerment was electric.

And hot.

Achingly so.

Valerie told herself to breathe. The last thing she needed was to pass out in Hutch's arms. Though, truthfully, there would be far worse places to lose it.

She stayed put. Her body, influenced by feelings too numerous to name, was speaking a new language.

Hutch's steely eyes commanded hers. Valerie allowed herself to be suspended in the space, absorbing the closeness as much as she absorbed the feelings it created.

Comfort.

Intimacy.

Safety.

Hutch had made a daring first move. He might have even been playing around in doing so. Still, the abruptness spurred Valerie, and she wasn't going to let the moment pass. She eased her heels off the ground, raising on tiptoes to close the space between them.

She touched her mouth to his, their lips meeting in shared pleasure. They exchanged a kiss that was as sweet as it was saucy.

Nothing sloppy.

Nothing forceful.

Just, oh, so right.

Chapter Twelve

HUTCH WAS PLAYING with fire.

He knew it. But he didn't know if Valerie knew it.

Regardless, she sure knew how to kiss. And also how to knock the wind out of a guy's chest in doing so.

Being around her made him playful and impulsive, which was why he had reached out to her in the first place.

And so had his lips.

This woman tasted like spunk and spontaneity, flavors Hutch hadn't tasted before. Usually, the women he dated— and therefore kissed—in Last Stand were local and safe. They were known commodities.

With Valerie, there was an allure of something different, something he didn't know he wanted to try. Yet even one kiss from her was intimate beyond his wildest expectations. Contact made his insides stir as if his emotions were being prodded with a barbeque fork. His flames were stoked.

Just like the rest of his body.

Revved and ready, he craved move, yet his manners reined him in and kept him steady on his feet. He stood mere inches from Valerie, feeling close to her and far away all at the same time.

In the quiet swell of emotion that lingered after such a perfect kiss, he was scared to move. He was thankful when

Valerie did, her sweet face retreating in slow motion reverse as she lowered herself onto her heels, opened her eyes, and simply looked at him.

Was she questioning what they had just shared? Had the whole initiation of being on her doorstep gone awry?

Or was she feeling what he was?

Something natural, something pure.

He had been knocked senseless by intimate acts with women before, but there was something entirely new in this experience with Valerie. He couldn't name it, couldn't put his finger on it. But he could feel it.

He slackened his easy grip around her waist, her hips moving in delicate response. One hand skimmed an inch of peekaboo skin that appeared then disappeared as she adjusted her posture before him. Even such slight contact was electrifying.

He just hoped she felt it too. Otherwise, his sensual intuition really was off-kilter.

Hutch could have stayed suspended in their coupled weightlessness for as long as Valerie wanted, though what he couldn't stand was the silence.

"That was unexpected."

"I know," she said with the same breathlessness he felt.

The unease that nipped at him disappeared. She experienced the same.

"I really came over to work on the walkway. I swear." Hutch raised his hand and crossed his heart, and Valerie's lip curled into a smirk.

He hammed up his actions, making a show of crisscrossing his chest with an X. Valerie released a tiny huff of air.

Then, she started to chuckle.

The sound was a melody Hutch didn't know he needed to hear. And he couldn't help but laugh too. A woman with whom he could share sensuality and humor was a rare combination indeed.

Valerie paused in between her laughter long enough to say, "You have one strange way of working, Bubba Hutchinson."

"And there it is." His reply was as smooth as her words.

"What?"

"Bubba." He enunciated the syllables, still a bit dazed he had admitted that piece of private life to her on day one.

"I like the way I say it better." Her words hung suggestively in the air, teasing him toward them.

"Then say it." His gaze moved to her lips, their color flushed pink as the words dripped honey sweet.

She repeated his name, the sound a siren call.

Weak in the knees, Hutch nearly lost it. Maybe he should explore this relationship, even if it was on borrowed time. He wanted to kiss her. He needed to kiss her.

"I don't know what it is," she started, "but you have some kind of way about you."

"I was just thinking the same about you."

"And if we keep standing here, neither of us is going to get any work done."

Hutch didn't miss a beat. "Work is overrated."

She smiled. "Touché."

He ran his hand across his forehead, as much to check for perspiration as to force his hand into moving in a way that wasn't directed at her. Even though his hands wanted to be all over her. "You know, there's no reason a single guy like me"—he wanted to drop that line in case there was any doubt—"can't keep coming to the doorstep of a pretty girl like you, hoping she'll answer."

"Is that what you're doing?"

"It's what I have been doing."

"And I keep answering." The look in her eyes was suggestive, beckoning him closer. He leaned further into her, keeping his voice at a whisper.

"Yes, you keep answering." His words trailed as they closed the distance between them. He wanted to bask in the radiance that tugged him close. But just as their lips were about to meet again, a car door slammed, jarring him back into the reality of the present.

Valerie stepped away as Hutch slackened his grip.

She cleared her throat. "Hi, Quinn," she called from over Hutch's shoulder. The intimacy they had just shared disappeared as quickly as smoke.

"Hi, you two." Quinn returned a wave before walking around her vehicle to the passenger's side. "I've got those books for you."

"Great." Valerie's tone didn't match the word's enthusiasm.

I know just how you feel. If Quinn hadn't interrupted, Hutch might have pounced on Valerie's signals in ways that didn't stop at a kiss.

But he was a gentleman.

He knew when to make a move. And when to put on the brakes.

Still, he had a golden opportunity. With Quinn's back

momentarily to them, he had to act fast. "If I come back tomorrow evening and knock on your door, asking you on a date, would you join me?"

Valerie raised an eyebrow. If she had been shocked by Quinn's arrival, this question hit her from left field.

"You. Me. And that pickup." He pointed over his shoulder. "I want to show you a good time by showing you a little of Last Stand."

Her face glowed as soft as the words in her answer. "Now how can I refuse such an offer?"

"You can't." He winked, sealing the deal. "How's seven o'clock?"

"I'll clear my schedule."

"Good." He took a step back, lowering himself into a slight bow. "Now, if you'll excuse me, I'm going to finish that walkway and send myself on home. Because if I don't"—he raised his upper body and met her gaze a final time—"then I might not make it home."

He waved to Quinn as they crossed paths. Then, he turned his attention to the walkway repairs. Thanks to the spark he shared with Valerie, he was fueled with enough fire to finish the walkway in no time flat.

Valerie Perry did something to him. And as long as he could make it to tomorrow night, he may just be able to experience it all over again.

"YOU'RE GLOWING." QUINN narrowed her eyes at Valerie. "I know that look."

"Do you?" Valerie tried to play coy with her feeling of puppy love. Or whatever it was that Quinn was seeing all over her face. She turned away and reached for the handle of the fridge.

"Don't try to hide it," she chided. "I saw you and Hutch getting cozy."

Valerie kept her back turned. "I was painting."

"Is that what you call it?"

She was going to need more than a sip of water to cool herself down. She opened the door and took a deep breath of frigid air. "So you know Hutch?"

"Everyone knows Hutch."

Valerie could sense sarcasm without even seeing Quinn's face.

She grabbed a fresh bottle of water. "What exactly does that mean?"

"That the Hutchinsons are well-known."

Valerie stepped back from the door and passed the bottle to Quinn. "Is that all?"

"Thanks." She paused to take a drink. "They're popular for being popular around town."

"Because of the barbeque market?"

"Yes. But popular from high school too. I was in the same grade as Cole. He's Hutch's younger brother."

"By two years, right?" Valerie remembered her lunch conversation with him.

"Right," Quinn confirmed. "So you know about the family?"

"I know a few things."

"I bet you do." Quinn held up a finger in playful admonishment, circling back to her original accusation. Valerie certainly had more history with her friends in San Antonio, but Quinn was able to read her just the same.

"I kissed him."

Quinn's mouth fell open. Silence settled before she snapped her jaw shut. "And?"

There were lots of ways Valerie could have answered.

And I never expected it.

And it was completely unlike me.

And his lips were sizzling.

All of Valerie's blood rushed to her face, and she covered her eyes with both hands as if she could shield herself from the sight of acting like a teenager. *What is happening to me?*

"I take it he wanted to kiss you too?"

The entire episode was indelibly stamped into Valerie's memory. "Yes," she confirmed. "He did."

"Wow." Quinn echoed what Valerie had been thinking the past hour.

"I know."

"So what's the problem?"

Valerie trailed her finger along the edge of the kitchen counter. "No problem."

"Well . . ." Quinn turned to the books she had brought, flipping one open on the kitchen counter. "If you're looking for advice from me, don't bother. I'm single, remember?" She added quickly, "Looking, but single."

"Is there much to look at around here?"

"Ouch. That's a little cold."

Valerie stilled her fingers. "I'm sorry. Really, I didn't mean anything by that."

But Quinn, in true librarian fashion, had an answer. "Actually, dating in a small town has its perks." She held up her hand and extended her thumb. "Number one, knowing people is a good thing. You can't get surprised, and you can't get duped."

On Valerie's first blind date after she moved to San Antonio, a coworker set it up, saying the guy was "between jobs" when she really meant "fired from his last one and living in his mother's basement." Valerie still shuddered at their awkward dinner—that she paid for—and the uncomfortable conversation when she realized his firing was as a result of sexual harassment claims.

That experience pretty much soured her on setups, so she hadn't accepted any more from people who she thought should know her better than they did.

"Number two, when you date in a small town, you know the families of the people you're dating." Quinn paused. "So you know a little bit of their history, how they operate, their level of commitment."

There was a lot rolled into that. Valerie had, coincidentally, met Hutch's whole immediate family at The Hut. There were guys she dated—even one quite seriously when she lived on the West Coast—who never introduced her to their family. So Valerie liked where this was going. "Continue."

Quinn held up her third finger. "People in small towns are hardworking. Reliable. They do what they say they're going to do. That's the nature of the place."

"True." Valerie couldn't argue with that from what she'd seen, especially with Hutch.

He followed through on commitments, which was why their paths had crossed several times already this week. That was a trait she couldn't say she saw much of in San Antonio: hot men just appearing outside her window and then recurrently coming back to knock on her door.

"Number four." Quinn was on a roll. "It's cheap to date here."

That made Valerie chuckle.

"No, really, like going out to eat is a breeze. No stuffy restaurant reservations, no long waits. And when it comes to outings, festivals, fairs, and celebrations are generally free!"

Valerie had to hand it to Quinn. "You're making a pretty convincing case."

"I did choose to move back to this small town," she said, "so I knew what I was getting into even before I arrived back here."

"And you came anyway?"

"Yes," she said with a smile, "I came anyway."

That someone as pretty, educated, and caring as Quinn would willingly return to her small town in her midtwenties spoke volumes about the kind of place Last Stand really was. Maybe there was more for Valerie to notice and understand than she had.

"Anything else?"

"Yes." Quinn looked as if she had been saving this one. "And it's a biggie."

That intrigued Valerie. "Hit me with it."

Quinn extended her pinky. "Charm."

"Charm?" Valerie repeated.

"Charm," she said again, this time more breezily, more

131

dreamily. "I can't quite put my finger on it." She brought her hand to the counter. "But I just know it. I went to college in San Angelo, transferred to Dallas, but I really missed the Hill Country. Not that west Texas doesn't have its advantages. And Dallas certainly has everything a person could want. Well," she backtracked, "almost everything."

"Let me guess. It was missing the charm?"

"Bingo." Quinn nodded. "You know it when you see it. You can feel it. It's not that other places and the people in them are lacking something, but it's that people here just have an extra layer. Something that's maybe a product of their upbringing or the landscape or the history of the place. I really don't know. I just know Last Stand has it. So I'm not opposed to dating here."

"But you're not dating anyone?"

"Not now." Quinn blew out a breath. "Library work has been keeping me so busy. Ever since I took over the job, it's all-consuming." She pushed back her shoulders and adjusted her posture, straight as a book's spine. "But I'll date when I'm ready."

Quinn gave Valerie a lot to think about. "I'm not exactly dating yet." The precise definition of what she was doing with Hutch eluded her. "But I am going on a date with Hutch tomorrow."

Delight danced in Quinn's eyes. "That's wonderful!"

"Is it?" She was glad to be talking this over with someone. "It's just not at all a part of what I expected would happen here." Those words were the understatement of the week.

Quinn answered Valerie's question with one of her own.

"Why wouldn't it be?"

Valerie mentally combed back through Quinn's list of small-town dating advantages. The charm, affordability, and reliability of the place and their people had been important ones. But agreeing to go on a date and actually having a sense of who the person was and who his family was became other advantages.

Quinn's points were convincing, and Valerie certainly held loyalty, commitment, and kindness in high esteem. Those were values she wanted in a partner.

Prior to today, she hadn't allowed herself to even consider the possibility of dipping her toe in the Last Stand dating pool. Her life had intersected with Hutch's, whether by chance, fate, or follow-through on his part. He kept appearing at her doorstep.

Each time, Valerie opened the door to him.

And wasn't letting someone in the first step toward a relationship anyway?

Chapter Thirteen

HUTCH HAD BEEN pouring over restaurant review webpages, social media comments, and dining guides for over an hour. With the lunch rush over, he justified time spent on his computer because he considered it research.

Research with a specific end goal in mind.

Keeping a pulse on the barbeque market as it existed in the digital world was not a concern his parents ever had, and it surely wasn't one his grandfather could have ever fathomed. During the market's early days, selling barbeque had involved pits, meat, and one man. Over the years, the business grew, and Hutch had watched it do so.

But its presence online wasn't an area of growth that anyone watched.

And someone should.

Hutch found plenty to read but even more to see. People shared photos of their food on social media like it was its own trend.

And it practically was.

Above-the-plate shots of barbeque platters, lunch combinations, and bowls of dessert made their food look especially appetizing. Seeing the grassroots ways people showcased and shared made Hutch swell with pride. He worked to make that food, and his family had built the place that was at the heart of all the fun photos he saw.

Yet as Hutch made his way through pages and feeds, one name appeared over and over as the giant in the barbeque scene of the Lone Star State: *Modern Texas*. The state's leisure and lifestyle magazine made it a point every year to devote one issue to barbeque. Not only did meat grace the cover, but the magazine listed a best-of-the-best list, ranking the must-see, must-try joints, no matter how small or out of the way.

In fact, it seemed like the more remote, the more *Modern Texas* loved to feature it.

Barbeque was big business in Texas, and the state's preeminent magazine made sure its readers were armed each year with the information they needed to chew their way through loads of ribs, sausage, brisket, and pork loins.

This year, Hutch intended for the family business to be on that list. It would be a major step toward jumpstarting a new wave of customers while injecting a shot of renewed local interest into the place.

The Hut had never had a *Modern Texas* food editor in its midst, at least not to Hutch's knowledge. But the magazine did so much with the joints they chose to feature that he would be a fool not to try and secure a visit. In addition to a glossy-paged profile, selected eateries could win awards, have on-site videos filmed, and be featured in the publication's annual barbeque road map. They even put together a playlist of songs to accompany those who took the trips.

This was marketing genius.

And he wanted a piece of it.

He tracked down the name of the editor, who was the

only full-time barbeque-focused journalist in the nation, as well as his phone number. He wrote it on a Post-it, affixed it to the bottom of his computer's keyboard . . . and then just stared at it. He couldn't bring himself to call right away, but as he searched, he kept seeing the bigger picture.

Big exposure meant big opportunities.

They didn't have the overhead to pay someone to monitor social media, let alone someone to seek out new opportunities for customer growth. Still, all it would take was one grand swing toward something like this, and if it worked out, they could grow their customer base enough to make up for less-than-expected sales earlier in the year. Even more than that, such widespread positive press could turn them around for years to come.

Of course, the downside was the food editor could hate The Hut. Even though Hutch stood by everything they made and would hang his hat on the work they did any day of the week, taste was subjective. After all, an editor had but one palate, and if that palate wasn't pleased, The Hut could be crucified in print and online in ways that would be indelibly stamped into customers' memories for long after an annual issue.

Ultimately, the rewards outweighed the risk. He just hoped the choice wouldn't burn him in the long run.

It might still be a long shot, but Hutch picked up the phone, summoning all his entrepreneurial bravado. He calmly dialed the number.

The phone rang several times before a man's voice answered. Once Hutch heard him say his name as editor on the other end of the line, there was no turning back.

"My name is Bubba Hutchinson, and I'm a third-generation family owner of The Hut in Last Stand, Texas." The next lines were make-or-break. "We're in a carnivore class all our own over here. And if you'll give me just thirty seconds of your time, I'll tell you why."

Silence held the line, and Hutch gulped to avoid a lump forming in this throat. He hadn't rehearsed anything, and now he was second-guessing his directness. This guy probably heard foodie pitches all day long.

Carnivore class? Really, what was I thinking?

But just as Hutch was getting ready to apologize and put his foot in his mouth, the editor responded. "Carnivore, eh?" Hutch took a breath and held it as he waited for more. "Son, you're speaking my language. What you got over there that I need to know about?"

And just like that, the door of opportunity eased open. Hutch wasn't going to blow this. On the contrary, he was going to keep his cool and work hard to convince this guy that a road trip was worth his time.

VALERIE COULD HAVE scrolled through shabby-chic photos all day on her phone. And if she hadn't been worried about draining her data plan, she might have spent the better part of Thursday doing that.

With no Wi-Fi in the bungalow, she was trying to reserve using the internet on her phone for important purposes only. That involved checking her email, accessing the weather app, and double-checking the charges on her credit card and bank statements.

Because even though she had money coming in while on vacation from work, she had plenty of money going out.

And watching that happen dollar by dollar was depressing . . . which was why it was so much easier simply to look at design photos and feel productive.

Though who was she kidding? When her thumbs were moving on the screen, she wasn't working. Not by a long shot. She might have tried to convince herself that idly looking at perfectly staged scenes from one lifestyle blogger after another was time well spent in the name of research, but she knew better.

It was stalling.

To keep herself from the temptation, Valerie turned off her internet access altogether and stowed the phone.

The more productive I am now, the more fun I can have later. With Hutch.

So once the touch-up paint dried in the living room, she staged the furniture and added the secondhand items. Everything looked so picture perfect that she snapped a few photos to text to her parents later. She had called them earlier in the morning to check in and share her progress, but seeing the room come together was going to make them shriek.

She just hoped that same reaction was one Penny could solicit from a buyer.

She looked around the space, hands on her hips as she took in her progress. "Not bad," she said. "Not bad at all." Her hard work made this happen, and the satisfaction she felt drove her to work even harder toward other projects.

She put in another solid two hours before she had to stop herself.

After all her work on the house, now she was the one in need of a little TLC. Before Hutch arrived at seven o'clock, she needed to bathe, scrub every bit of errant paint from her skin, and freshen up enough so that she didn't look—or smell—like century-old wood and semi-gloss paint.

Although, from what she knew of Hutch, a scent like that might just be pheromonal to him. She smiled at the thought. "He's not like other men I've known," she mused on her way to the claw-foot tub. He was unpredictable and persistent. He was present in a way that forced her to not only see him but to strip back her hesitation and indecision. After all, he got her to say "yes" not only to eating at a barbeque market but also to a date.

Who was she in Last Stand? Herself? A version of her grandmother? Or someone else entirely?

Funny how, at different times and in different places, people could uncover new knowledge about themselves.

Valerie wasn't nervous about seeing Hutch. With other dates, her nervous reactions were pretty predictable. Her mind would consider the logistics, her body would flush, and her stomach would flutter.

None of that was happening tonight.

Instead, Valerie was comfortable in a way that was almost unfamiliar to her. As she leaned over the tub and twisted both brass knobs, she flicked her fingers beneath the steady stream of Hill Country spring water that ran through the tap. She was cool and calm, her thoughts collected into a what-will-be-will-be mentality. She was ready to go with the flow.

Once the water warmed to her liking, she stripped off her work clothes and plunged into a comforting soak that softened her skin and rejuvenated her muscles. She had no idea what the evening with Hutch would hold, but as she enjoyed a respite unto herself in the cozy space of this place, she'd be ready for it. Because already during her time in Last Stand, she was ready for anything.

HUTCH HADN'T BEEN on a first date in months. His last attempt at one left a bitter taste in his mouth for all things romantic.

It was one he wanted to forget.

That was because he thought he was going out with a woman who was single.

But it turned out she was married. Separated, but still married. The I'm-going-home-after-this-to-sleep-in-the-same-bed-as-my-husband-even-though-I-hate-him married.

He wouldn't touch it with a ten-foot pole.

It had been Cole's fault since he was the one who set Hutch up with the woman in the first place. He had conveniently forgotten to share that bit of complicated personal dirty laundry with his older brother. When Hutch confronted him the next time, he just shrugged.

Shrugged! Of all the ways he could have responded . . .

But tonight's date with Valerie would be completely different. The spark he felt between them the day before told him so.

He took his time striding up the walkway of the bungalow. The cowboy boots he wore this evening made firm clacks against the flagstone, different than the dull thuds from the soles of work boots he wore the day before.

With each step, he admired his handiwork on the walkway. There were no more visible cracks, no sign of a recently fallen tree. Farther in the yard, new plants freshened the curb appeal, though, if this were his place, he'd lay some new sod and flank the front entrance with plants to match those by the mailbox. The house might also benefit from some gutters.

Hutch's mind was always on work, whether at The Hut or around town. But tonight, he would relax.

He took a deep breath, raised his hand to the front door, and triple knocked his arrival. It didn't take long for the door to swing open.

"Hi, Bubba."

He still smiled at that. "You know not many people get to call me that."

Valerie tilted her head, her long, freshly combed hair cascading across her shoulder and framing her face in a way that was more perfect than the *Mona Lisa*. "Then why is it that I do?"

Hutch pushed aside his focus on her physical attractiveness. No reason to hold back his answer though. "Because you say it genuinely." He flashed back to his school-age years and the torment he received from classmates who had a field day with his given name. "There's no teasing. No charades."

Valerie eyed him from behind lashes so long he wondered why he hadn't noticed them before. Full and lush, they hung like curtains above irises the color of bluebonnets. They were his favorite flower, and he hoped there would still be a fair spot of them around the lake to which they were heading.

"No charades," she repeated. "Not when it comes to me." She lifted her head, shaking back her hair ever so slightly and looking him straight in the eyes. "What you see is what you get."

And, at that moment, Hutch felt like he was looking directly into the sun. Reflected in Valerie was a brightness and intensity that melted his insides and made his knees nearly buckle. Heaven help him, unless they walked to the truck soon, his body might just melt into butter and pool right there at her feet.

"Let me grab my purse." She turned, giving him a moment to collect himself. When she returned with a purse strap hanging over her shoulder, she added, "By the way, I got something for you." She held out her hand and as Hutch looked to it, he saw a perfectly poised miniature barbeque pit cast in brass. "I thought of you when I saw it."

Hutch plucked it carefully and raised it to the light. Squinting, he examined it. "I've never seen anything like it."

"Neither had I. It's a pencil sharpener." She leaned close to him, her body grazing against his as she pointed to the side of it. "I thought you might be able to use it at The Hut."

"That's a great idea."

"A conversation starter with people, if nothing else."

"They sure don't make them like this anymore." He was tickled by the idea that vegetarian Valerie would buy something barbeque centric for him. "Thank you."

She shrugged as if the gesture was no big deal.

But it was. Actions spoke louder than words, and this woman had just impressed him with hers. She was kind and thoughtful in unexpected ways.

"Are we ready to go?" She swung her purse in front of her and reached for the doorknob.

"We sure are."

Valerie had caught him unaware but in a good way. He was also assured through her pep and enthusiasm that she was ready for the evening as he had planned for them.

He walked her to his pickup, opening the passenger-side door without even thinking twice about it.

"Thank you," she whispered, her voice seemingly surprised at the gesture. For Hutch, chivalry was never overrated. There were certain things a man did for a woman. His grandfather had taught him that, and he had further learned from a lifetime of seeing his father in action as well. Texas men, after all, had reputations to uphold. And proper manners and good graces were never ones to be taken out of the equation.

Especially not in the presence of a beautiful woman.

"I'm going to stash this here." He reached over to open the glove box and placed the pencil sharpener inside, taking a moment longer than necessary to linger and read her body language.

She didn't move her knee.

She didn't shuffle her feet.

She didn't recoil.

She sat confidently forward, as if daring him to stay

close.

And, boy, did he want to do just that.

"Ready for a ride?" he teased.

"Let's do this." Her eyes sparkled more brightly than Texas topaz.

He eased back, closed the door, and took the long way around the back of his pickup to let himself in to the driver's side. He needed that moment to himself to bite his lip, pump his fist into his hand, and let out the bit of fire that was lit inside of him in anticipation of this date that was already placing his emotions on overdrive.

Chapter Fourteen

"SO WHERE ARE we headed?" Valerie settled in to the surprisingly comfortable front seat of Hutch's pickup. The interior smelled like hard work with its mixture of leather and tools. Earthy scents seemed to swirl all around Hutch, though in such close—and closed—proximity to him, she now detected something new.

Cologne.

A woodsy, alluring scent of something spicy and warm triggered a stirring in her chest and an intense desire to move closer to him. She adjusted her seat belt, pulling the shoulder strap away from her chest briefly so that she could get some air. Proximity to Hutch was going to her head in a way it shouldn't. Because this was the beginning of a date, and she was in no position to act on any physical impulse at the moment.

Hutch stayed steady at the wheel, one hand resting comfortably near the top while the other casually steered from the bottom. "I thought we'd drive out to a spot that has some of the best views in the Texas Hill Country."

"Oh? Which road?" She turned to look at Hutch, his broad shoulders and ample forearms on full display, even though they were covered by a crisp, starched shirt. He cleaned up well.

Hutch said the name of the farm-to-market route, but the number didn't mean anything to Valerie. What did mean something were the details she was noticing about Hutch. While he was preoccupied with driving, she was able to study him in ways she hadn't previously, even when they were face-to-face at her doorstep.

His profile was classically handsome with deep-set eyes, a natural slope to his nose, and a chiseled chin. But it was the bright laugh lines around his mouth and eyes that gave his face a natural look that drew Valerie in.

Plus, Hutch's effort at presenting himself didn't go unnoticed. In fact, his long sleeves and fresh pair of blue jeans made Valerie question her own style choice. Not that she had a lot of options in what she packed for the two weeks here. She hadn't planned for date ware, so she'd improvised with a simple but flattering V-neck tee in her favorite shade of yellow and some khaki shorts that were at least more on the tailored side than anything else she had worn.

"Will we be getting out of the truck?"

"Your choice." He raised one hand to point with his thumb to the truck bed. "I packed some dinner for us. So we can eat in the cab or picnic outside."

Valerie hadn't expected that plan and couldn't hide her surprise. "You actually prepared food?"

"Semihomemade," he dismissed. But she couldn't ignore Hutch's thoughtfulness, especially when he added, "And, don't worry, because I packed vegetarian things for you."

In all of her history with dating, she never had a man cook for her. Even eating a meal from a cooler was more of a personal touch than she had gotten from men in the past.

Her dates made reservations. Used their credit cards to pay for parking garages. Rarely did they even ask if she had any dietary restrictions or preferences.

She said softly, as much to herself as to Hutch, "I hardly know what to say."

He laughed. "Don't say anything until you see what I did. It's nothing fancy."

"I'm sure it's perfect." Because there was something genuine about Hutch that she observed every time she was with him. He didn't put on airs, and he didn't pretend to be something he wasn't. And that was magnetic to Valerie.

The magnetism intensified thanks to their proximity. Nearness made her want to be even nearer, and an image she never quite understood before slid into her mind. A woman riding shotgun not in the passenger's seat next to a man but sidled right up next to him in the middle of the bench seat as close as she could get. It always seemed silly when she saw this in movies or music videos. The cowboy and his girl sandwiched together like that in the cab of a pickup had always looked so fake, so posed. Why would anyone sit like that?

Yet she wanted nothing more than to do just that. She reined in the urge to slide next to Hutch, touch his arm, and kiss him sweetly on the cheek for his gestures so far. Rare was the guy she knew who even drove a pickup, and for those who did, they were pristine trucks with bucket seats and interiors that never felt the wear of manual labor. They weren't a working man's vehicle like the one that Hutch drove.

Point blank, the guys she knew simply weren't like

Hutch.

She thought about kissing him again, just a quick yet sincere peck on his cheek to let him know that she appreciated him.

But she held back. She wasn't impulsive by nature, and she certainly didn't want to alarm Hutch. Instead, adjusting her position by crossing her legs, she tried to sit tight. Valerie pressed her knees together, trying to keep her limbs from being restless and her longings in place.

Get a hold of yourself. Because if Valerie didn't stay in control, she might just lower more than her emotional guard with Bubba Hutchinson.

"WE'RE GOING TO take a left up here." Hutch's pickup was far too old for a GPS system, so he had fun calling the directional shots himself.

Valerie played along. "Turning left," she echoed in her most robotic voice.

Hutch made a dramatic gesture of turning on the blinker, even though there wasn't another vehicle in sight along the FM road. "Now we keep going straight."

Valerie uncrossed her legs and leaned slightly forward in her seat. "This looks like a pretty out-of-the-way place to me."

"That's the idea." Getting away from prying eyes and curious gossipers was the goal. Public dating in Last Stand should come with warning labels. *Warning: if you go out with me, there will be rumors circulating.* That was what it felt like in a small town. His married date lived in the next town over—if he believed what she said—so at least he didn't have to face direct scrutiny for that. He just continued to beat himself up personally for not being more careful.

But with Valerie, he didn't have to be careful. He could just be honest. So far, his time with her raised no red flags, and there were no uncomfortable moments.

Unless he counted her bombshell admission of being vegetarian smack in the middle of a barbeque market. But he had already forgiven that culinary sin.

Still, she had proven herself as a woman who would try things. So Hutch was taking a gamble on this evening's choice of a date, and in doing so, he hoped it was unique enough to make an impression.

"This is kind of the middle of nowhere." Valerie turned to admire the view from the truck window. "It sure is beautiful."

Bluebonnets were in the final week of their spring season, but their characteristic color still shone brightly against the green pasture grass. "We're lucky these wildflowers are still out."

"I'll say." Valerie reached for the manual window. "Mind if I roll this down?"

"Be my guest." Hutch clicked off the air conditioning before reaching for his driver's side window and churning the crank. With both windows in the cab now lowered, fresh breezes blew in like a crosswind, whipping Valerie's hair and teasing Hutch's nose with smells of her wafting perfume. The scent mingled with the rich fragrance of the bluebonnets.

Valerie reached up and smoothed her hair, holding it into a side ponytail as she lifted her head and inhaled deeply. "Those flowers smell incredible. It's been a long time since I've smelled fresh bluebonnets."

"You can smell them every year out here." It was a simple aspect of country living that Hutch loved. "All the hills are covered. Some years, the rains bring more of them than the one before."

"So it must have been a good year for rain?"

It didn't take a meteorologist to see that. "Yes. It sure was a good year." The hills were fertile, the cattle were happy, and the ranchers were making profits.

"Can we pick some of these? I'd love a little bouquet to brighten up the living room back at the house."

"Now, you know picking the Texas State flower is illegal?"

Valerie guffawed. "Only in state parks, right?"

"So you know your state laws." She was correct on that point.

"I'm not ignorant." She slackened her grip, and soft strands of her hair flittered loose, teasing Hutch as they lifted and lowered in the wind.

"Right." He swallowed hard, trying hard to keep his eyes on the road.

"So we only have to worry, then, if a game warden finds out." She turned her head gently. "And I don't see any of those around here."

"I don't either. Out here, it's going to just be you"—he paused as he brought his eyes from the road to Valerie—"and me."

The moment of eye contact between them was as hot as the setting sun, and the potency he felt in sharing those words was just as intense.

If Valerie felt it, too, she turned her gaze away from him before he could read further into it. As quickly as a tide of interest rose, it receded again.

She looked out the window. "My grandmother liked antique roses. But I remember a summer when the house was full of tiny containers of wildflowers." Her voice sounded as far away as her thoughts. "Little milk glasses and bud vases full of ones she must have gathered from somewhere."

Hutch sensed a memory mounting. "What else do you remember?"

Valerie snapped her head forward, closed her eyes, and rested her head against the back seat. Hutch rounded the bend in the dirt road that would take them to his grandfather's lake. Valerie's chest lifted and lowered as she took a deep breath. "The vases had these little bumps of a dot pattern all across the middle." She raised one hand from her hair, as if reaching to touch the recollection of them. "Like large Braille."

Hutch knew what she was describing because his mother had a milk glass collection. "Scalloped edges?"

"Yes." She nodded, her eyes still closed. But her face was alighting to further memories. "There was one with a little crack." She traced an imaginary curved line in the air. "My grandmother repaired it with Krazy Glue, but I can still feel the rough spot in the shape of a banana." Her eyes popped open in surprise, and she whipped her head toward Hutch. "Do you know she made banana bread every week? Saturdays were for baking . . ." Her voice trailed, and her enthusiasm halted just as quickly as the memories had started.

Hutch held the silence in case Valerie wanted to start again, but when she didn't, he decided to say something to let her know he had been listening. And to let her know it was okay to share memories. "I like banana bread. Not as much as pudding," he added a plug for his mother's signature dessert that patrons of The Hut adored. "But I like it."

"I'm sorry. I don't even know why—"

"Hey, don't apologize." He wasn't going to let her feel guilt for spending a few moments in a walk down memory lane. "It's natural for you to think about your grandmother."

"Not for me," she started, a bit of edginess in her tone.

He wasn't sure what to make of that, but he could share the reality of his own experiences. "I think about my grandfather, even though he's no longer here."

"What occupies your mind the most?"

"Duty, mostly."

"Duty?"

"Doing right by him. Working hard not to destroy what he built in the business." Hutch tightened his grip on the steering wheel. "Or strangle my brother in the process."

"Sibling rivalry?"

"Something like that." He paused before adding, "I just want to keep the place going, you know?"

"I can understand that." Valerie placed her hands firmly on her knees as the truck slowed. "Are we getting close?"

He pointed to their destination, the dead end of the dirt road at the top of a hill that yielded spectacular views of the undeveloped Hill Country. There was shade on one side of the lake that started there thanks to a grove of beautiful live oaks. He eased the pickup under their wide limbs, angling it just so in order for them to have a perfect view of the setting sun if they sat on the down tailgate. "We've arrived," he announced.

Valerie brushed back her hair with her fingers, the strands relaxing around her shoulders as she unhooked her seat belt. "This is beautiful."

"Wait until you see it in three-hundred-and-sixty degrees." He unclicked his own seat belt and insisted, "Let me get your door." He moved in one fell swoop out of the cab and rounded the bumper to her side of the pickup, spreading on the charm thick as gravy. "Allow me."

"Thank you." Valerie swung her legs toward Hutch and held onto his outturned palm as she stepped onto land that had been in his family for three generations. Her lotion-covered skin was smooth to the touch, and the sun's rays stretched across the wide sky, accentuating Valerie's pretty features. There was a shiny hint of gloss on her lips he hadn't seen earlier, and the glint from the sun made her mouth appear lit by rose-gold rays.

Valerie tried to take a step forward, but Hutch didn't move. He was frozen in admiration of the way her features were framed against the backdrop of the natural sky. "You look so pretty."

She leaned forward and the lips that drew Hutch's initial attention now continued toward him. His body knew what to do.

He leaned into Valerie as well, their bodies bending close in the shadow of the still-opened door to his pickup. He reached one arm to brace himself against the cab, and with the other he circled her waist, drawing her toward him.

He had no intention of kissing Valerie in that moment. It wasn't part of any plan.

But Hutch was happy to place plans on hold.

They shared an affectionate kiss that was as sweet as the wildflowers that surrounded them.

Warmth spread through every inch of Hutch's body, hottest in the areas of skin that were touching Valerie's.

This girl made him sizzle all over.

Yet with a gentle release, she pulled back, looking up at him with a teasing challenge. "I bet you say that to all the girls you bring up here."

Hutch kept Valerie in his arms, not wanting to release contact when it felt so right. As familiar as this place was and as often as he came, this wasn't some act. He needed Valerie to know that. "I don't bring women here. Never have."

But now that he'd brought Valerie to this place, he wanted to show her just how special this act was.

He kissed her again and again as the sun sank lower in the springtime sky. They lost track of time together. And, for once, Hutch had no words.

Chapter Fifteen

V ALERIE SWUNG HER legs from the back of the downed
pickup tailgate, pumping her feet in steady rhythm.
Carefree as a child on a swing, she said, "I think I could sit
here for hours."

"I like the sound of that." Hutch reached for the cooler.
"But you might get a little hungry in the meantime."

"You think of everything."

"Let's hope." He also slid forward a reusable grocery bag
filled with a few disposable items. He started unpacking an
array of food, paper products, plastic cups, ice, and a thermos that would be used in a meal for two. There wasn't a
formal picnic basket, but, actually, she might have been
worried if there had been. After all, a guy owning a wicker
basket outfitted for romantic picnics would have been a
warning sign that he was someone who made such excursions
a routine.

And from her interactions so far, she doubted that was
the case.

Besides, based on the look of the well-worn cooler, the
two red SOLO cups he procured, and the roll of paper
towels they were going to use as napkins, Hutch wasn't
exactly an expert in picnic readiness. Sure, he had the bases
covered. But he wasn't wooing her with Magnolia Home

style.

But he was going to woo her with vegetables.

And that alone brought as big of a smile to Valerie's face as any fancy basket would have done.

He lifted a series of containers in rapid succession. "I brought a tomato and cucumber salad. We also have coleslaw from The Hut that you liked."

"You remembered!" Valerie clasped her hands like a kid embracing a fireworks display.

"I don't forget things that matter." Hutch paused, and Valerie's heart skipped a beat.

Are we still talking about food?

He continued. "Here's some corn dip with roasted peppers and black-eyed peas."

I guess so.

Hutch popped the container tops.

"That looks really good." Valerie hadn't seen that dish on The Hut's menu. "Who made it?"

"I did." He drew his eyebrow downward. "Are you surprised?"

"I am." She dipped her chin sheepishly. "Do you cook?"

"Yes." He reached into the grocery bag and pulled out a final container. When he lifted the lid, the hearty, buttery aroma of homemade country biscuits wafted on the air. "And I bake."

"Really?" She spread her fingers and fanned them against her breastbone. Her voice was soft, almost disbelieving. "You made those?"

"Just a handful of ingredients. No yeast. It's simple."

"I've never made homemade biscuits," she admitted.

"Once you do, you'll never go back to store-bought." He passed them to Valerie. "Help yourself."

"I will." She picked one of the drop-style biscuits, its flakey, floury exterior crowning what she knew would be a soft, delicious center. Simple foods like this were perfect by themselves.

"I've got some dewberry jam if you want it."

Well, maybe she had made up her mind too soon. Perfect foods, after all, could be even more perfect with delicious condiments. "Yes, please." Her stomach was in happy, hungry knots.

Using the tailgate as both bench and table, they shared a lovely, simple meal that was unlike any other first-date experience Valerie had ever had. "Let me get this straight. You trim trees. Your family owns a barbeque market. And you can bake?"

"Some things." Hutch held up his hand, as if wanting to put the brakes on too-thick domestic compliments. "I can't bake everything."

"You can bake these." Valerie took a satisfying bite.

"My grandfather always made these biscuits, and when he first sold barbeque, he'd put one or two in a small paper sack for customers. It was kind of like a little bonus for people who stopped by his shack."

"No seating back then, right?"

"Right." Hutch nodded. "So biscuits were an easy side dish. When my parents expanded the place, they continued serving biscuits for a while. But then my mom started baking bread, and customers wanted that."

Valerie swallowed her bite before asking, "Have you

thought about bringing the biscuits back?"

"On the menu?"

She nodded, holding up the last half of her biscuit. There was a hint of sweetness to the batter that made it unique. "Yes. An official market offering."

"Actually," he began with a hint of hesitation, "my brother's been pushing for a revamping of the menu."

"And?" she prompted, taking another buttery bite.

His forehead creased in contemplation. "And I actually hadn't considered the biscuits again." The wheels of a fresh idea churned across his face. "But maybe I should." The more he talked the idea through, the more his confidence built. "You know, I'm going to mention it to Cole. He might just go for it."

"Good for you." Valerie was pleased that she was able to help Hutch with a decision, indirect as her influence may have been. "Because these really are delicious."

"Thank you." Hutch finished his before pouring her a refill of sweet tea he had brought in the thermos. It felt good to sit, share, and talk.

"Now, after this . . ." Hutch placed the SOLO cup back on the truck bed. "We've got a few other mouths to feed."

"Oh?" Valerie's ears perked up.

"Them." Hutch pointed to the lake, and she squinted to see tiny bubbles of air popping atop the placid water. "The catfish are already waiting for us."

"We're going to feed catfish?" Valerie barely knew what catfish looked like, let alone what to feed them. "Do I need to save some of this biscuit?"

Hutch laughed. "No. That's for you," he insisted. "But I

did come prepared. They're going to eat that." Hutch motioned to a sack of what Valerie had previously thought might have been potting soil in the corner of the pickup bed. "Those are catfish pellets."

Valerie wrinkled her nose. "That's a thing?"

"In the country, everything's got a thing." He looked back toward the lake. "And these fish like this floating variety. The pellets look a little like dog food, but they must taste like a million bucks to them. You'll see."

"So I'll know if the fish are happy?"

"Oh, you'll know."

They finished their tailgate picnic as the sun put on an evening show, reddening the western sky in bands of color so bright the contrast of hues against the green grass and blue flowers was almost surreal for Valerie. She took back her assessment that country living looked dull. From her vantage point in this moment, country living looked brighter and more colorful than any style of living she had seen before.

Once lakeside, she tossed food to the fish, watching their gaping mouths encircle the pieces and suck them below the surface. They disappeared as fast as she could toss them, and it was a surprisingly fun experience.

She laughed with Hutch as they stood shoulder to shoulder, the ease of a comfortable day surrounding them.

HUTCH COULDN'T HAVE asked for a better first date. He had little time to plan, but taking Valerie to a location that was special to him turned out to be a good move.

Often, he was so busy with tree-trimming jobs and responsibilities at The Hut that he underestimated the effects of being still. The embrace of nature, the pace of an evening outdoors, and the company of a woman were relaxing on many levels.

As evening fell, the color drained from the sky. The glow of fireflies descended then, punctuating the evening in magical perfection.

Valerie held out her hand, catching a pair of the unique bugs. "I saw these for the first time the other night."

"You haven't seen fireflies before?" Hutch must have not heard her right.

"I have. Just not as an adult." She twisted her hand as the harmless bugs explored their temporary landing pad. "In the city, I don't see them. And for all the years I lived out of state, I never came across them. I hadn't seen them since the final summer I spent in Last Stand."

"They are pretty fun." Hutch held out his hand to match Valerie's, wanting to get close to her any way he could. His skin grazed hers, and the two bugs now explored both their hands in curious ways as their orbs continued to light. They really were incredible little creatures.

Valerie bit her lip. "So many memories have come back to me since I've been here."

Hutch suspected as much from what she shared earlier. "Is that a good thing?"

Valerie didn't immediately answer. Perhaps she was searching for the right words. "It's nice to have them to hold on to." After she spoke, one of the fireflies took flight, followed shortly by the other. She brought her hand back down to her side.

Hutch did the same, their contact broken. "Memories are funny things too."

"How's that?"

"Well, there are all these things that a person is supposed to remember. The big stuff, you know?"

Valerie nodded.

"But when it comes down to it, all a person really remembers sometimes is the little stuff."

"Like what?"

"Like, certain foods. Laughs. Outings. Sometimes just a scent. Or a sound." He eased his posture to the left, grazing her shoulder with contact. "A touch."

Valerie didn't move her shoulder, and the warmth of her skin felt good even through his shirt. "I'll be remembering lots of things from this week in Last Stand."

The dose of reality forced Hutch to swallow hard. "That's right. The house you're staying in is being sold."

"Hopefully sooner rather than later." Valerie shifted her weight, breaking their contact.

"Why the rush? I thought you had two weeks off from work."

"I do." Valerie took a step forward, putting distance between her and Hutch. Her eyes scanned the lake. "But if I can get this renovation project complete, there's no reason I can't go back earlier."

No reason? The words hit Hutch worse than a fist to the chin.

"If I go back early, I might be able to cash in a couple of vacation days. And since I've been spending money here on the renovation, that extra bit could really help." She rattled on, but Hutch couldn't keep his focus on her words. She sounded so distant.

During the past few days, he had pulled attention away from the restaurant to help her. He worked himself ragged in doing so. Then, taking Valerie to family land, treating her to a picnic meal, helping her on the bungalow, Hutch had folded her into his life this past week.

Sure, he cared about money. But he cared about people and experiences more. Didn't Valerie?

"So there's *no reason*"—he emphasized her words—"to stay here another week?"

If Valerie was sensing the undercurrent of his question, she made little indication. "I just mean that I've got to consider things back home—"

"Home." He looked around his family's private property. Did she even understand what a big step it was that he would take her to this extended home of his? Showing it to her meant something to him. "What does home even mean to you?" he asked simply.

Valerie straightened her posture. She seemed to consider the question before clearing her throat. "Home is a place you live."

"Is it?" That was the wrong answer as far as Hutch was concerned.

"It can be anywhere. Here. There." Her flippant words weren't what Hutch wanted to hear. "It's just a place." Valerie folded her arms across her chest.

Their conversation had taken on a whole new tone.

All of Hutch's life, home was the community and the

people in it. "Do you really think home is just a place?"

"Yes, a place," she repeated, turning to square off with him. "I'm in a place that was Val Perry's home. She may have given it to me, but it's not mine." Her eyes were deep with alarm, though her words were firm. "It's a house, but it's not my home."

Hutch had grown up in Last Stand. He knew the definition of place, but he also knew that place could be claimed. Home could be staked.

But a feeling of home had to be won.

He searched Valerie's face, studying it for some sense that she wasn't planning on leaving Last Stand the moment the house sold and never returning. He wanted to see the spark he felt reflected in her eyes.

But Valerie's face, soft as it appeared and kind as her eyes were toward him, didn't convey the desires that matched Hutch's. Nor did she say as much.

She added, with no emotional fanfare, "Selling that place has always been the plan."

As she stood before him, there was zero promise of a future. She wasn't making a move to talk about a long-distance relationship, even though San Antonio wasn't that far away. Did she not want to at least give it a shot to see if her city sensibilities could be stripped away and she might enjoy connecting with rural life and someone like him?

Apparently not.

Valerie was a fish out of water from the moment she stepped into Last Stand, and though Hutch thought that he could help her find her way and swim in the sea of happiness that he called home, he couldn't.

Because she couldn't.

Valerie Perry wouldn't be happy in an out-of-the-way place like this with someone as plain as him, and she was saying as much.

"I think it's best I take you . . ." His voice trailed before he uttered the word *home*.

Valerie nodded. "That's probably best." Her voice was harder now.

They walked to the pickup in silence. The curtain of nightfall darkened their movements. The evening that began with promise ended with a whimper. They left the lake with little fanfare, like two actors exiting a stage that had already dimmed.

And maybe that was what Hutch failed to see earlier. This was an act. Valerie's time had an expiration date, and she wasn't going to fight to extend it in any way. She was going to walk away from this just as she had planned. Nothing he had done—or could do—would change her.

Chapter Sixteen

THE RIDE BACK to the bungalow was long. And silent.

Valerie had made a mistake by agreeing to this date with Hutch. She let her guard down, and she thought that by doing so she could not only have a little fun but also explore something that was tugging inside of her. She couldn't name it and couldn't quite put her finger on what pulled deeply enough for her to yield to a kiss and accept an invitation of intimate outdoor lakeside time together, but the evening that started with a spark ended with a fizzle.

For what it was worth, though, she enjoyed all but their last conversation.

She slid back into the cab of Hutch's pickup, longing for a rewind button. There was a hollowness inside of her, and she could focus on little but staring out the truck window. Outside was a pristine evening sky and sparkling stars, but inside the cab, there was silence.

Valerie shut her eyes, trying to make sense of the physical and emotional void. Was her conscience trying to tell her something? And, if so, was it even worth the risk to listen to it?

The words she tried in her head all sounded wrong. It wasn't until they got close to the bungalow that Valerie found her voice enough to say, "I want you to know that I appreciate this evening."

Hutch eased the truck to a halt near the mailbox.

You can't even pull into the driveway?

Hutch looked straight ahead, his lips pursed. She waited for some type of response. But all Hutch did was press the brake. He didn't even make a motion toward shifting the truck into park.

Valerie could read between the lines.

"So you don't want to talk?"

He confirmed as much with his lackluster reply. "There's not much more to say." Then, true to his work ethic, he added, "If you need something else with the house, call me."

The house. Valerie's heart sank.

Maybe she had misread his cues all along. Had he truly been interested in her? Or was he duty bound by house calls she had a hand in forcing?

Valerie didn't have answers. All she had instead was a fading connection to someone she never expected to connect with in the first place.

She reached for the handle of the truck, pausing just long enough to give Hutch a window to say something to make her stay.

But he didn't.

Their fieriness dimmed as distance stretched between them. She swung the door closed. The metal's gong-like reverberation stayed in her head as she walked away.

Inside the bungalow, Valerie's heavy-footed steps were as painful as lead weights. Valerie was used to being alone. But tonight, she wasn't just alone. She was lonely. Hurt. Disappointed.

Annoyed and agitated.

A little at Hutch.

And also at herself.

Later, when she tried to sleep, restlessness took hold instead. There were too many emotions to sort, and her mind raced a mile a minute. The sandman eventually came, but even when morning broke, it didn't bring a clear head.

Rise and shine? No way.

Valerie pulled a pillow over her head, her whole body lacking energy. Still, she couldn't stay buried all day. There were tasks that needed to get done.

So she employed the same technique she used in the apartment when she absolutely needed to go into the office. She simply made one deliberate move after another.

It was an adapted rise-and-shine approach, but it worked.

She stumbled to the kitchen, wiping sleep from her eyes before opening the cupboard. As she reached for a mug against the back wall, a bright glint of milky, white glass caught her eyes.

At no point during the week had she seen this in the cupboard, yet plain as day, here it was. She closed her grip around the patterned bumps, the same as she had described last night to Hutch.

So she hadn't imagined the milk glass vase after all.

She dusted its sides and turned it over in her hands.

This was Grandma Perry's.

All along, her mind had been spooling through actual memories lodged deep in her subconscious. All week, small ones were surfacing beyond her control.

Valerie admired the craftsmanship of the stout antique vase. She hefted it in her hands, lifting it up and down to feel the weight.

They don't make them like this anymore.

Her fingers felt their way to a small crack, repaired long ago. The curve was the shape she remembered.

She smiled to herself. Her mind hadn't betrayed her. She was right in this memory all along.

She brought the vase close, siphoning love from the woman it represented. She barely remembered what a hug from her grandmother felt like, but in that moment, she tried to recall.

Grandma Perry had loved Valerie. Her home spoke to that, and the memories they made within it did too. No matter that their time was limited; what they lacked in quantity was balanced by quality. The summers spent with her grandmother were infinitely precious. Those memories were worth saving.

Just like this vase.

Valerie's heart swelled. She inhaled, letting her chest fill slowly before releasing her breath in a controlled exhale. She repeated until she was sure her heart wouldn't crack like the vase.

She placed the milk glass on the counter, centering it by the base. Tall, stately bluebonnets would have looked perfect in it.

She and Hutch never did get around to picking bluebonnets.

An aggressive knock on the door brought Valerie back to the present. And if she needed an accelerator to that, leave it to Penny Bristo.

The women blew in like a hurricane when Valerie opened the door. Stepping inside, her hawk eyes immediately assessed the changes. "Mailbox area has some curb appeal. Plants look better. Walkway is smooth." Penny's voice commanded attention more quickly than an auctioneer's, sucking the air of nostalgia from the room.

Are you a real estate agent or garden inspector? Valerie bit her tongue and instead ushered Penny in. "Good morning."

"Good morning," she returned, her voice terse and almost flustered by the interruption. "But something's got to be done across the front. Color or window boxes or something."

"I plan to hire a power washer." That had been on Penny's original list, and after giving it some thought, Valerie had decided that it was in the realm of what she was prepared to do.

"That's a good start because it's going to need paint."

"Paint?" The word hit Valerie like a swift slap. "On the exterior?" Painting interior walls with the help of a step stool were one thing. But the entire exterior of a home? That was a task bigger than Valerie could handle.

"Buyers will want it, trust me." Adding that last phrase was like trying to soften the sting after a bandage was ripped from human skin. Words couldn't help at that point. "And it's better to do it now before showings get lined up."

"But I thought you said you already had interested buyers."

"Some." Penny spoke with authority, but Valerie sensed from her tone that it might be wavering. "But the more options we have, the better. Besides, when I post these next set of photos, I'll start to drive more interest." Penny walked through the space, visually appraising the work Valerie had done while fast-talking through all the work Valerie had yet to do. "I can wash a few of the pictures in photo filters so the paint job outside is less noticeable. Digital doctoring is a real estate agent's best friend," she said with a wink.

No way would she post anything dishonest. "I don't want to—"

"Dupe people?" Penny was a step ahead of her.

"Yes." She had taken the words right out of Valerie's mouth.

"Please, honey." She waved her hand as if she were shooing a fly. "Let me ask you a question. You wear makeup?"

"Not at the moment." She didn't have time for much that morning.

"Fine." She pointed to her own cheek that was clearly layered by a heavy application of blush. "I do."

You don't say?

"And I don't consider makeup a way to dupe anyone. Instead," she continued with the confidence of a Mary Kay spokeswoman, "it's a way to enhance what we naturally have."

Enhance. Camouflage. Apply like someone straight out of clown college. So many spunky comments were on the tip of Valerie's tongue. Penny had a way of soliciting that, yet her forthrightness was exactly what Valerie needed in order to secure a sale, especially with a buyer who might be on the fence about purchasing. So Valerie pushed aside reluctance in order to follow along with Penny's train of thought.

"All I'm saying," she continued, "is that I'll filter a few things to enhance what's here." She spun to face the living room, letting out a happy squeal as she did. "Now this! Shabby chic, my heart!" Valerie had no idea what that even meant, but the combination of high-pitched sound and non-confrontational words said she had done something right in Penny's eyes.

"Do you like it?"

"Nailed it!" Penny grabbed her phone from her purse and immediately started snapping photo after photo. She paused only long enough to change the flash before snapping again.

Valerie just tried to stay out of her way.

Penny moved with purpose all around the space. "Let me see what it looks like if I shoot from here." She crouched next to one of the new table lamps that Valerie had bought with Quinn. "This angle into the kitchen is really going to enhance the look of the space." Then she clicked and clicked.

The woman sure did take a lot of photos.

"Is the powder room in order?"

"Yes." Valerie gestured that way. After she had taken her bath in preparation for meeting Hutch, she had carefully folded each towel, wiped down the tub, and made sure none of her personal toiletries were left within view. And with the new mirror hung above the vanity, it was in pristine shape for a photograph.

Penny poked her head into the small space but didn't flip the wall switch. "The natural light is perfect in here." Early morning rays streamed through the only window, drawing pretty patterns of illumination on the tile floor and bathing the room in a pleasing glow.

"No filter needed on this one." Penny clicked and clicked.

"Will you upload these today?"

"That's the plan." She held her phone at arm's length, making a few adjustments to the settings before diving back into paparazzi mode. "People in town will look at the house during the week. But buyers from out of town drive in on Saturday. So I want to have something online to give them a landing space."

"Fair enough." Valerie was leaving the process in Penny's hands.

Well, not quite *all* of the process.

Penny kept her phone at the ready as she narrowed her focus out the living room window. "Now about this back-yard." And as her real estate agent enumerated improvements Valerie hadn't even considered, she could feel her own self-confidence drain away.

She had gotten so much done, yet all she heard was how much there was left to do.

"You said you planned on power washing, right?"

"*Hiring* a power washer." Valerie knew her limitations.

"So when's he coming?"

Valerie's mouth went dry. She bit her lower lip.

"I know a guy." Penny was already scanning the contacts of her phone. "I can get him here tomorrow."

"Thank you." Valerie knew this would be her expense, and hopefully Penny's contact was reasonable.

"Now what about help with painting and general yard maintenance?"

Valerie could use that, but with every new addition to

the list, she saw dollar signs before her eyes.

Penny held her thumb over the screen of her phone. "Do you need recommendations?"

The least Valerie would do was take down a few names and numbers. But even as she did so courtesy of Penny's encyclopedic list, she wasn't sure how comfortable she'd be just cold-calling someone on the spot and then negotiating a job. Penny could help in some aspects, but she was hired as an agent, not a renovation foreman. Valerie ultimately needed to stay in charge of what was done on the property, though what she could use was an expert in local know-how and resources.

And there was one local name that she did trust, even if she didn't end things with him on the best of terms.

The house quieted the minute the door closed behind Penny. Valerie grabbed her phone and scrolled to Hutch's name, staring at it as his final words the night before rang in her ears. He had, after all, left an open invitation for her to call for this very reason.

But did that mean she should?

Preoccupation will get you nowhere. Valerie had muddied the waters with Bubba Hutchinson, but stepping past that to reach out to him might be a way to move forward. Their conversation would be about business since Valerie had a renovation job to complete. They both valued work.

And communication was a part of that.

Besides, Valerie wanted to have a more respectable conversation to at least soften how things ended between them.

Swallowing her hesitation and pushing aside her pride, she sent a quick text message to Hutch.

Chapter Seventeen

FRIDAYS AT THE Hut required all hands on deck.

The place was like a meat mecca, crawling with locals, out-of-towners, and travelers just passing through. But Hutch didn't care how hungry mouths showed up at the barbeque market.

He only cared that they did.

And as the hours stretched on and the cash register kept steady tabs for the sales, he had a hard time rationalizing what he'd learned about profitability so far this year. Business today was great, uncharacteristically so. There wasn't even a festival, three-day weekend, or major event that he could point to as the reason for the influx.

Customers just came in waves. Hungry, big-ticket waves.

Totaling the sales at the end of day would be a fun task, and Hutch could already see the dollar signs in front of him.

"We're out of brisket. And ribs," Cole said. Those were the worst words he could hear. "Don't promise any more for orders over the phone."

"How many pounds did you put on the pit this morning?"

"Same as last Friday."

"But we've got a lot more customers today."

"Which is why we ran out earlier than usual." Cole's sarcasm sizzled.

"So are you going to add more sausage?" They had to have something to serve customers.

"Already did." He was ready to turn his attention back to the pits outside when he added, "Try to push the chopped beef and pulled pork. We've got plenty of that for sandwiches." And while that was true thanks to their saucy mixtures that could be reheated and seemed to taste even better with a little bit of age, not everyone wanted a sandwich.

"I can only sell so much of that," Hutch insisted. "My problem's out there." And Cole cut out of sight before Hutch could say another word.

Customers were a blessing, but disappointing them by not having a full menu was a curse. No matter how many years Hutch spent in the food service business, it never got easier.

After a few tough conversations and having to talk customers into various second and third options, Hutch was finally ready to flip the sign on the front door to *closed*, kissing goodbye a day full of both promise and disappointment.

Before the *Modern Texas* editor arrived, they were going to need to reinventory their meat locker and make some tough decisions about upcoming preparations. Old plans weren't working for new days. And, as much as Hutch hated to admit it, Cole might be right. As long as they were rethinking the amount of meat they put on their pits, they might rethink the amount of items on the menu.

Hutch stood near the register, picking up the brass pencil sharpener Valerie had given to him. He turned the object over in his hand like a worry stone, a bittersweet reminder of their time and the promise their connection had held. He dropped his shoulders, lost for a moment in thought.

The sound of a crashing pan from the kitchen snapped him from his daydream. He put the pencil sharpener back in its place but heard no further ruckus from the kitchen. So, it was time to find Cole.

He was determined to move forward, and heaven knew it was the right move for the business, too. He told his brother as much.

"Glad to hear you've had a change of heart."

Hutch didn't care to think of it like that. "Listen, I don't want a full change until after the editor comes. It's just too risky to make an overhaul when we've got this possibility looming."

"And is it looming? When did he commit to coming?"

"Commit," Hutch repeated, chewing on its meaning, "is such a strong word . . ."

"Spill it," Cole demanded. "Did he commit or not?"

"He said next week. But"—this was the part that made Hutch really nervous—"he didn't give a definitive day."

"We just have to bring our A game every day of the week." Cole cracked his knuckles against his palms one at a time, more like a football player getting ready for a play than a barbeque boy getting ready for a food review.

Still, he had to admire Cole's readiness. And, because of that, he was also ready to make a small concession. "I'll agree to you trying one new side dish." He held up a single finger. "Not on the menu board, but let it loose on a few locals next week. Then, if they give it the go-ahead, we can mention it to the editor when he comes as something experimental."

"Just one?"

"Actually, there will be two additions."

"Two vegetables?"

"A vegetable," Hutch corrected. "And biscuits. Grandpa Bubba's biscuits." Of all the decisions he'd made today, this one felt the best.

"Fine. Corn casserole."

"See?" Hutch smiled, the shine of compromise surely lighting his face. "That's going to pair so well with Bubba's biscuits."

If the way forward for their fifty-fifty ownership was brotherly feuding with occasional coming together on decisions like this, Hutch would take that as a win.

Cole disappeared back to the pits.

With his brother out of sight and the demands of the workday easing from his shoulders, Hutch checked his phone and saw a text message from Valerie.

Got any tips on envisioning a better backyard at the bungalow?

He tapped his foot against the floor as he read the words again. What was she asking?

Do you need ideas? Or manpower?

Her reply was instant.

Manpower.

Hutch stared at the screen. This girl was hot then cold, intense then calm. He shook his head. He should sideline his personal feelings and let his business sense kick in. After all, there were some post oaks in her yard that could be shaped, and The Hut could always benefit from more wood.

Brody and I can trim some limbs.

He hit SEND before he could reconsider.

Thank you! I'll pay the going labor rate. And all the wood you can haul off is yours to keep.

So her mind was on work. Not that he could fault that trait in a woman.

Maybe they were each playing the same game.

Hutch's insides were a cocktail of emotions. Still, he couldn't deny the flutter in his chest and his quickening heartbeat when he'd seen Valerie's name appear on his phone. That drove his reply as he typed out a reset to their first day of interaction.

If you want to see me, you should just say so.

There was a long pause before a message pinged back.

I want to see you.

Hutch smiled. Was she sincere? Hard to discern through text, though when he rewound memories of all but the last portion of their night, the preciousness of their quality moments together fossilized. This budding relationship was a rare discovery, and it was worth saving.

I'll be there at three o'clock.

She added one more request.

Know any woodworkers? Reclaimed barn wood as window boxes? I'll provide the materials and order food for everyone from The Hut.

That was one way to support business.

On a Saturday in a small town, groups could mobilize in no time flat. Especially if there was work—followed by a party. Food was a good start.

So anyone who comes gets a hot meal at a little backyard

evening shindig?

He had to wait several minutes.

Whatever you say.

Well, it was an affirmative even if it was an on-the-fence one. And just like that, Hutch had a full Saturday, complete with evening plans and, as far as he was concerned, a fresh opportunity with Valerie Perry that would at least give them both the possibility to end on a different note.

"YOU'RE AN ANGEL for spending your day off with me." Valerie passed a bottle of homemade all-purpose cleaner to Quinn.

"Beats sitting at my place." She had arrived first thing Saturday morning to help Valerie with details of getting the place ready for buyers to see. On tap was wiping down the insides of closets, the cupboards, and skimming dust from the baseboards that seemed to settle in overnight. Maybe she shouldn't have slept with the windows open.

"I doubt renovation and cleaning work is more fun than sitting at home."

"If you think being at home alone is more fun that doing something, then you haven't spent enough time in Last Stand," Quinn insisted before popping a slice of fresh Hill Country peach into her mouth from the small tray of fruit she had brought with her. She had picked up fruit, kolaches, and coffee from the town's German bakery opposite the Carriage House.

"How's the peach?" Valerie raised her coffee cup and

took a sip before reaching for a slice of fresh-off-the-tree produce.

Quinn swallowed. "Delicious."

That small taste made Valerie crave something more.

What I wouldn't do for a smoothie. If only I had packed the blender.

She missed a lot of comforts at her apartment, like Wi-Fi and a dishwasher. There were also personal effects she should have packed to make her feel more like herself, like her organic hair conditioner that could have tamed all her annoying flyaways. Or her pink-and-black polka dot cozy socks with the little rubber bottoms that would have made padding around on the old tile floor more comfortable. Being away from familiar things was starting to add up for her.

But it wouldn't be for much longer.

"I really appreciate this," she told Quinn. "And, remember, when I'm back in San Antonio, you're welcome there any time."

"I might just take you up on that."

"I hope you do." It would be wonderful to have Quinn come to the city. "I need to properly thank you for all the help this week."

"It's been fun."

"Still, I owe you. And I will pay you back." That was a promise Valerie aimed to keep.

Quinn turned her immediate attention back to work. "What is this stuff anyway?" She squirted the liquid from the bottle into the living room and gave it a sniff.

"Vinegar and water. With a drop of lemon essence oil."

It was one of Valerie's favorite simple cleansing mixtures that she used on practically everything.

"I just buy blue stuff in a squirt bottle. But I like the smell of this."

"Nontoxic, nonstaining, and all natural." Sometimes, Valerie was completely confident in her choices.

Then, there were other times.

"Now, after we finish inside the house, let's talk about the backyard."

That whole space scared Valerie. It was overgrown and ill tended. "That's why Hutch is coming."

"What time? And how many people is he bringing?"

"Three o'clock." Valerie filled Quinn in on the work-to-pleasure impromptu party. "If you have friends who are around with nothing else to do, invite them. Especially if they're in the market to buy a house."

"Aren't you worried about too many people coming through here?"

"Who said anything about anyone coming inside?" That was Valerie's plan at least. "They can enter through the side fence. Everyone stays out."

Perhaps it wasn't the most inviting thing to do to guests. But with such pleasant spring weather, having people mingle in an outdoor space that she provided was a good start to being hostess after the work party. Plus there was the promise of all-you-can-drink beverages and hot food from The Hut.

Quinn had a socializing idea of her own. "If everyone's outside, I think you need a fire pit."

"I don't have a fire pit." And Valerie wasn't about to

needlessly purchase one.

"You have a barbeque expert, coming with a crew, descending on your backyard. I bet if you tell the guys you want a fire pit, they'll build you a fire pit." She made it sound so simple, as if people just came together and did what others asked.

But as they got to work and Valerie reflected on Quinn's words, she wasn't completely off the mark. Hutch—and, by extension, others in town—had already proven that they could help when neighbors needed it. And although Valerie wasn't a local, time spent here sure made her feel like one.

As the hours passed, Quinn turned out to be as expert an interior cleaning and organizing maven as she was when it came to design. The librarian in her was good for so many things. Just as they were finishing with laying new liner in the kitchen cabinets, the sound of truck engines announced new arrivals. Valerie checked her watch.

Three o'clock. On the dot.

"How many do you think they are?" Quinn stood to peek out the window.

"I hope an army of them." Valerie joined her. Pushing back the curtain, she added, "And it looks like there is."

She recognized Hutch's truck. Brody got out of a different vehicle, along with someone else she didn't recognize. There were two guys in Hut T-shirts who stepped out of a flatbed work truck. Then, a car pulled up with one man and two women.

"Is this a parade?"

"Might as well be." Quinn shrugged.

"How many of these people do you know?"

Quinn started pointing one by one and offering names. "Cole is the one carrying the ladder." She identified the man with the same brown hair as Hutch.

"I recognize him from The Hut." Although, out of context, Valerie would have had a hard time placing him since she'd only seen him once.

"The other guy is from there too," Quinn added. "Brody and Logan are just a couple of friends of the Hutchinsons. I was in the same grade as Logan. With Cole too. Brody is Hutch's age." She rattled off details with such ease that it was hard to keep up.

"And them?" Valerie pointed to the women, one about her age and one possibly older.

"The couple from the front seat lives in the neighborhood. One of the women in the back is someone I work with. She lives a few streets down, not far from them." Quinn draped her arm around Valerie, coolly saying, "Word travels." She winked and smiled knowingly.

"I don't know if I'm going to have enough food." Valerie ran her hand across her forehead.

"Then you better ask those barbeque brothers to up the order."

Valerie weighed the cost of food against what she imagined was the going rate for manual labor. If she could appeal to everyone's stomachs, she might avoid having to tap too far into her wallet. "It feels like the whole community is coming out for this."

Quinn stood at attention beside Valerie. "As long as you're here, you're a part of this community."

"I'm only here temporarily." Valerie felt a pang of guilt.

"It doesn't matter." Quinn pulled back. "You're still here. And for however long, people are going to help. That's how communities thrive. We help our neighbors. Shoulder the hardships. Celebrate the accomplishments."

Valerie understood that in theory. She had just never quite seen it unfold in practice.

Quinn shrugged. "It's called commitment."

Commitment.

The word rang in Valerie's ear. It was too late to second-guess anything.

"Is that part of why you came back to Last Stand? I mean, of all the places you could go with your degree—"

"I wanted to be right here," Quinn confirmed. "I value this place. And the people." She looked out the window before lowering her voice. "But some people here work harder than others. See Bethany over there?" She nodded with her chin. "I really don't know how much work you'll get out of her. She's a talker."

Valerie smiled. Ability to hold a proper conversation was an important value. "Talking's fine by me."

"Don't encourage it too much." Quinn winked. "Oh!" Her tone changed on a dime as her eyes locked onto Bethany's movements. She reached into the trunk of the car, looped her hands around a couple of bags of groceries, and started up the walk. "She's got food!"

Valerie saw something unmistakable at the top of the bag. "She brought marshmallows?"

Quinn stepped back from the window and admitted with a hand-in-the-cookie-jar look, "I might have said s'mores would be fun to make tonight."

"I don't have a fire pit," Valerie reminded her.

"But you might." Her voice held promise.

Before she let the curtain fall into place, Valerie caught glimpses of people unloading all manner of the tools she needed, including a wheelbarrow and a power washer. Maybe Penny had called one of these guys anyway.

She'd sort that later. Because right now, an extreme makeover crew had descended onto the bungalow's lot, and Valerie couldn't wait to see what the next few hours brought.

"AROUND HERE . . ." Hutch eased the ladder onto the side of the house and braced its bottom into the soft dirt. "People help people." He stood back once the ladder was steady and looked at Valerie with a smile. "That's just how it's done."

"Where am I? I feel like I should pinch myself."

"Last Stand," Hutch said simply. "Your grandmother settled here for a reason. It's a good place to be. It's home." He couldn't resist adding that last bit of pitch for his hometown.

Especially given the bitter way their Thursday evening had ended.

Valerie pushed her hair from her face. "About that idea of home—"

"And there you are!" Hutch's voice rose as his attention focused on some activity behind Valerie.

She pivoted.

"Nod! Come here, boy." He leaned down, patted both palms on the tops of his jeaned thighs, and gave a short whistle. The dog raced over to him, tail wagging and loose tongue ambling with each stride.

"We have a new helper?" Valerie crouched down and held out her hand.

"Allow me to introduce the neighborhood's most friendly canine." Hutch scratched Nod's head, rustling the fur between his ears. "That's a good boy." His fingers moved back and forth as the dog's eyes spoke to pure bliss while his tail picked up speed.

"He's a happy dog." Valerie reached to stroke his side, and almost immediately Nod's balance shifted, his back curved, and he flopped onto the ground. He wiggled and wrestled against the grass with all four paws up in the air.

"I think he's begging for a belly rub." Hutch bent lower to oblige.

Valerie did the same, and they both gave Nod the undivided attention he wanted. "I wasn't expecting this boy to be part of the crew."

"Nod likes to be involved." Clearly, the dog enjoyed attention. "Which is why he was here for our tree-trimming job on Monday."

"So this is the dog." Valerie softened even further. "You're the one who caused All. Dat. Twouble," she said to the canine in a saccharin voice. She pursed her lips and cooed at the dog with a face only a pet lover could understand.

Hutch stifled a laugh. "Is this how you always talk to dogs?"

"Cute ones." Valerie cooed some more, and Nod was just eating it up.

"So . . ." Hutch stood and wanted to bridge the introduction. "Now you understand why I couldn't let a tree fall on this guy. But," he added quickly, wanting to make sure Valerie understood the full loop of why Nod was here today, "his owners are the ones who came in the silver car. They live a few streets back, and when they were in The Hut yesterday for lunch, I told them about everything. They insisted they wanted to come help because they felt bad."

"That's really sweet." Valerie gave Nod a final pat on the tummy before she stood and rejoined Hutch. Nod rubbed his nose against the grass and wiggled one last time before he flipped back over. His tongue wagged, and his bright eyes seemed to thank them both for the impromptu belly rub. Then, he turned to find another set of willing hands to give him some love.

"Hope you don't mind him hanging out here for the day."

"Not at all. It's nice to see a friendly animal face. And I'm grateful for the help." Valerie glanced again at Nod. "And grateful you were able to spare that tree falling on him."

"Me too," Hutch agreed. "Nod's one of a kind. He's sort of a neighborhood institution."

"I'm beginning to understand that." Valerie smiled. "In fact, I'm beginning to understand a lot about Last Stand."

Hutch liked those words.

Very much.

Because he liked Valerie.

Very much.

He had only known her a short time and he didn't know where all of this was going. He didn't have to know. Because sometimes a person didn't need to envision the end result to simply enjoy the ride.

Chapter Eighteen

T HE REST OF Saturday unfolded in a series of projects. Valerie directed some, like the need for power washing and back fence clearing. Carlos, from The Hut, was super handy when it came to quick woodworking projects, so he whipped up a couple of window boxes from reclaimed lumber, thrilled to take home what he hadn't used. Then, he and Brody were able to complete electrical hookup for some garden lights to frame the front flowerbeds.

And every house needed a fire pit. Evenings were too pretty in this part of Texas to let them go to waste. The crew of guys worked to clear and level a rounded area in the backyard, and they used some extra bricks that were previously piled along the back fence to make an attractive focal point.

Cole had cut an old piece of grill that they laid across the top of the bricks. Nothing fancy, but with some extra flagstone left over from the front walk repairs, the new addition tied perfectly in to the rest of the house.

In several hours' time, the backyard had been tamed.

"I can't believe you guys built a homemade brick fire pit." Valerie stood over the work, openly staring.

Hutch shrugged. "It wasn't hard." With the right materials and so much available labor, it was a super quick project.

"But it makes a big statement back here. And now there's a reason to use this space."

"I'll say." Valerie clasped her hands.

"And we have to try it out tonight," Hutch insisted.

"Not a problem there." Cole had been in charge of bringing food from The Hut to feed this hard-working army. "Care to help me inside?"

"Lead the way."

They entered through the back door, which was the first time Hutch was getting a true taste of the interior. Furniture was perfectly arranged and tastefully ordered. "This is beautiful."

"Thank you. But it's small."

What it lacked in size it made up for in charm with windows that optimized the light and sensible built-ins that made the place cozy.

"It's smart," he countered.

"I hope buyers think that way." She sighed.

"You might think everyone wants big spaces. But there are plenty of people who prefer quality of the space to the size of the space." At least he did.

"You think this has that?"

Hutch pointed toward the kitchen, taking steps in that direction. "Cherrywood cabinets."

"I have no idea."

"That wasn't a question." He ran his hand along the smooth finish, admiring the grain. The quality craftsmanship took his breath away.

"You like it?"

He beckoned her closer with his voice. "Come here."

Valerie walked soundlessly toward him. Hutch held one hand against the cabinet and, with his other hand, invited her to do the same.

Slowly, she raised her hand next to his. He guided her hand against the wood as if they were going to feel a heartbeat. Grazing her skin, her body heat transferred to him in a brief but exhilarating jolt. "Feel this."

Valerie wrinkled her forehead.

"What do you feel?"

She stared at the wood for an overlong moment before her eyes slid to meet his gaze. She didn't speak.

Hutch didn't want to either. Instead, he held his breath and stayed suspended in the moment. This—just being—was what he relished in life. Responsibilities slid away. Time stood still. And side-by-side companionship appreciating the beauty of surroundings was all that mattered.

Sometimes, the world moved so fast he forgot how much he liked slow.

Slow movements.

And a slow burn.

Their hands rested side by side, their chests rising and falling with their breaths. Chemistry strung smooth as a guitar chord between them.

Hutch leaned in, taking his cues from her close proximity. But her hand dropped, and her whole body pulled back.

She turned, pinching the fabric of her shirt and fanning her chest. "I think I need something to drink."

A stiff drink might help them both. "What do you have in here?" Hutch moved his hand from the cabinet to the refrigerator handle. Swinging the door open, he gave Valerie a few seconds of privacy as he scanned the rows of cooling beverages. "Want something alcoholic or nonalcoholic?"

"Non."

"Water?" He grabbed a bottle by its neck and held it high enough for her to see above the door.

"Perfect."

He twisted the cap before passing it to her.

"Thanks." She took a long drink. "Aren't you going to get something?"

What Hutch wanted wasn't in the fridge.

And no manner of liquid refreshment could quench the thirst he felt at the moment. He tried to listen to his heart; he tried to lead with his emotions around Valerie. But when he did, she pulled back. Every step he thought they took in the right direction was countered by one in the opposite direction.

"I'll get something later." He turned to the trays of food, swerving into familiar territory with focus on something that didn't tie his insides into knots.

He was good at food service. After all, food never played games with his heart.

A HUMAN BRIGADE passed alcoholic and nonalcoholic choices hand over hand down a line that stretched from the bungalow's indoor refrigerator through the edge of the living room, out the back door, and across the prim backyard to the newest outdoor showpiece—the hand-built fire pit.

Penny was definitely going to have to update the sales

listing once she heard about this.

The evening's spring weather was perfect. Laughter seasoned the air, and thumbs popped aluminum tabs in a rippled sound wave before everyone, sweaty from their labors, took a long drink.

"This is just what I needed." Quinn tilted her head back as if resting her neck against a pillow of air.

"Want to sit?" Chuck and Waverlee had brought folding chairs and positioned them around the fire pit.

"I'm good for now."

"Long day." Valerie could use a moment to put her feet up, but she wanted to get the food served before she did.

"What's on the menu tonight?"

"Whatever Cole brought." She was only vaguely aware of some of the items. The rest of the aluminum trays and foil-wrapped foods were a mystery. "Do you trust him?"

"With barbeque? Yes."

"And with other things?" It was hard to get a read on Quinn and Cole. When Valerie had seen them laughing together at one point earlier in the afternoon, she had a fleeting moment of playing matchmaker between them. But who was she to meddle?

Especially considering she wasn't an expert in navigating a relationship of her own.

"When it comes to both those barbeque brothers, I'll admit they have the gift of grill," Quinn said.

"Touché." Valerie nodded toward the fire pit and raised her beverage in the air.

Quinn joined her for a dull clink of their cans as the rest of the work crew gathered around the fire pit that looked like it had always belonged in the backyard. Nod bounded underfoot, stopping whenever he suspected he was close to getting a scratch behind the ears.

Quinn obliged. "That's a good dog."

"He really is." Valerie had no complaints with the canine. She had, after all, been quite wrong about him in the first place. He wasn't a troublemaker or rabble-rouser.

And neither was Hutch.

Even though she originally thought he was a piece of work.

And now?

Valerie slowly traced the rim of her beverage can. Once. Twice. Three times around. She paused and circled in the reverse direction, the steel leaving a cold indention. Suddenly, Hutch slid two fingers between his teeth and cut the conversation with a high-pitched whistle. Heads turned at attention.

"I'd like to make a toast." He raised his beverage high in the air, signaling everyone else to do that same. "Here's to hard work we'll remember, and friends we won't forget."

Clinks and "here, here!" cheers made the rounds, voices spreading joy before Cole announced that the food had been properly warmed on the fire pit. Paper plates and napkins were at the ready. But everyone wanted to see what Cole had cooked up before they started piling their plates high. He unwrapped bundles of pepper-crusted beef brisket, smoked sausages, and saucy ribs that made everyone who wasn't a vegetarian moan.

And that was everyone but Valerie.

"Don't think I forgot about you." Cole waved her closer

to the pit, where Hutch was already standing. She joined the group, standing between the brothers so that she could get a proper look at a tray Cole pointed to on the grill. "I prepared something special that I think you're going to like."

"Oh? You know I'm vegetarian."

"I do know that." Cole gave a curt nod, looking briefly to Hutch.

Had they talked about her?

Cole gave her no time to consider the question. "And because you are vegetarian, I'm eager to get your feedback on this." He pushed one hand into a silicone mitt and lifted the foil from atop the tray.

Heat rose in curls, swirling and dancing in the air as the evening breeze brought an unmistakable smell to Valerie's nose. "Is that—"

"Better not be meatballs," Hutch said.

"What's wrong with meatballs?" Cole's jaw stiffened.

"You know how I feel about those." Hutch stood his ground. "They're a totally inferior product. I have standards when it comes to—"

"Hush." Now it was Cole's turn to cut in. He lay the foil to the side of the fire pit before bringing the tray closer for Valerie to examine.

But she already knew what delicious food held that aroma.

"Brussels sprouts!" Her taste buds somersaulted as her mouth watered.

But someone else's mouth didn't have the same reaction.

"Devil cabbages," Hutch muttered.

"Hey! That's my food you're talking about."

But the ridiculous humor of the name settled into her, and she chuckled. "Did you just say—"

"I don't like them."

Quinn stepped closer. "Why are you talking like Dr. Seuss? And why do you have to like them?"

Even in the low light of the evening, Hutch's face flushed a storybook shade of red. He pushed his aluminum can to his lips rather than say anything else.

"Thank you, Cole."

"Now this is a recipe I think customers might like. These roast beautifully on the grill. All it takes is a little oil, some sea salt, a couple of—"

"Enough talking." Now Valerie's stomach was joining in the chorus moans of the other guests. "Let's dig in!"

Everyone enjoyed the outdoor spread. Nod even ran by with a bone.

As darkness slipped in, Carlos and Brody made sure the timers on the new ornamental lighting lit at the right time. There were a few extras that Valerie got from the hardware store that were added to the backyard, so the entire exterior of the bungalow was bathed in soft illumination. As day turned to night, the fireflies arrived right on schedule.

The magic of seeing them—even for several nights in a row—hadn't yet worn off on Valerie. Their presence was as spectacular tonight as any other.

She drifted to the edge of the property line following some, and when she came to a stop with her hand outstretched, one landed in her palm.

She stayed still to keep the gentle creature in place. Only when she took her eyes from the scene for a moment did she catch sight of Hutch, who was smiling as he watched her.

HUTCH STROLLED NEXT to her, the glow of the firefly's light shining between them. He wanted to say something, but he held back. Seeing Valerie experience joy in her surroundings and revel in the magic of fireflies was an experience that didn't need words.

But Hutch still wanted to talk to her. He just didn't know what to say.

She broke their silence. "Have you tried any of the s'mores?"

Hutch held up two fingers.

"Guilty." Her voice sounded sultry and seductive against the evening air. "They were good. Maybe the best part of the evening."

No, food wasn't the best part of the evening.

Not by a long shot.

"*This* is the best part of the evening. Seeing you . . ." But Hutch couldn't find the right word to finish.

Valerie's hand rocked to one side, and the firefly took flight. "Good-bye lil guy."

For a brief moment, Hutch heard the words directed at him. It was only when he followed the trail of light that he snapped from the silly, self-imposed misunderstanding. Yet good-bye was on his mind. Eventually, Valerie would be saying it to him.

"Good-byes are hard."

"I know." Her hand dropped to her side. "I've said lots

of them in my life."

"Always definite?"

"Pretty definite." She wrapped her arms around herself.

"Are you cold?"

She shook her head. "No. I'm actually feeling . . ." Now it was her turn to search for the right word.

"Take your time." Hutch wanted to give her all the space she needed. To think. To talk. To figure out what she wanted to say.

Because what he wanted to say was *don't go. Stay here. Let's make something of the chemistry I know exists between us.*

But he stayed silent in respect to whatever thoughts Valerie was trying to form.

She said, "You know I'm leaving, right?"

He stuffed his true feelings deep down.

He said none of what was in his heart but masked his desires with words of stoicism instead. "I know. So I guess that means we're about done here." Hutch turned, leaving Valerie to herself. *It's where she wants to be.*

Hutch headed toward his group of friends, leaned next to Brody's chair, and fished a cold bottle from the icy cooler at his feet. He twisted the top and took a long drink of a beverage that he hoped would dull emotional pain he wasn't in the mood to feel.

Chapter Nineteen

VALERIE HAD PLENTY of practice at shelving and compartmentalizing her emotions. A childhood spent moving from house to house had taught her to do just that.

Every time her parents announced a new move, she would empty her closet, clear her shelves, and pack her own belongings. At school, she never told her friends she was leaving.

She just never came back.

Good-byes seemed too hard.

After all, without good-byes, she didn't have to face others' hurt. She had learned to guard herself in this way, creating a fierce independence. Clean breaks were a survival mechanism.

They helped her move on.

Then.

And now.

Or so she hoped.

Saturday night had ended poorly with Hutch. That much was clear. It was clear in his eyes before he turned away from her.

But navigating feelings had never been part of the plan. The plan had been to come to Last Stand, rehab the bungalow, and sell it.

Quickly.

She couldn't afford the upkeep, the taxes, and maintenance when she had her apartment and all the associated expenses back in San Antonio. Besides, the bungalow was in the best shape Valerie had ever seen it.

In just a week's time, the house was transformed. Power washing gave the exterior new life, and the combination of fresh plants, garden lighting, and the backyard fire pit made the small space a cottage oasis. Inside, the shabby-chic details hit all the right notes and accented the original charm.

Online, Penny had drafted a beautiful description of the property, complete with phrasing straight out of the type of books Valerie had borrowed from the library. She was also calling the property "move-in ready," a phrase that delighted Valerie as much for its sales angle as for the truth of what it suggested: that the place was really ready to be someone's home.

Today was Sunday, and Valerie had cleanup work from the backyard gathering. She also wanted to add some mulch to the front beds and trim a few of the bushes into more rounded shapes. Every little bit of improvement, she figured, would help increase the value of the property's first impression.

Yet memories of the way the prior evening ended with Hutch were still green.

As much as she tried to compartmentalize, it was difficult to do because she was used to being the one who walked away.

But, last night, the roles were reversed.

Hutch's leaving was an image she couldn't shake. Nor

could she ignore the emptiness in the pit of her stomach, an unquenchable absence of unfinished business that seemed to chew on her from the inside. Did the friends she left behind in childhood feel this way?

A more recent encounter wound its way into her subconscious. Earlier in the year, she had several dates with a banker from San Antonio that she thought were headed in the right direction. But at the end of dinner one night, her guy announced, "We need to talk."

Never a good sign.

He tried to soothe Valerie with a salve of empty phrases. But one that was meant to lessen the emotional pain had cut deep instead. "You're a nice person, but you're just not opening up." He had accused her of being cold and distant.

At the time, she thought he was so off base.

But, now, judging by the emotions swirling inside of her like the contents of a beverage blender, perhaps there was some truth in the words he spoke.

Valerie's life in one place had always come with an expiration date. Timing controlled her emotional response to the people around her.

It was happening again.

But habits were hard to break. She came to Last Stand to close a chapter of her life.

And she was going to do that.

She needed to offload this house as a final good-bye to her grandmother, an act she never got to perform in person because her grandmother passed in her sleep without any of her family members around her. So placing the house in good hands would be a proper send-off for the place that

Grandma Perry loved.

To that end, Penny had lined up several showings over the next couple of days. The ball was rolling, and soon Valerie could head back to San Antonio where she belonged.

HUT'S KITCHEN SERVED as command central for Monday morning's new menu trials of Bubba's homemade biscuits and Cole's corn casserole.

"Valerie really liked the brussels sprouts. Are you sure I shouldn't have tried those?"

It was too late for little brother to be asking for big brother's opinion. "This is what we're going with today. Remember, it's not on the chalkboard menu because we don't want to overcommit."

"Right."

Cole ran through the kitchen like a running back while Hutch coached. "We're just going to try a quick launch today. No pressure."

"I know that." Cole pulled two steaming trays of casseroles from the oven.

But who was Hutch kidding? Even he knew there was pressure for these dishes to sell, even if the burden was all self-imposed.

Luckily, Hutchinsons had food sense in their DNA, so scaling the process of one-dish home cooking to commercial capacity were challenges the brothers could accomplish.

When it was time to launch, they asked a couple of regular, trusted customers to taste a sample along with their meal and give their verbal feedback, which was all positive.

A thumbs-up.

The okay sign.

Several customers grinned after tasting their first bites.

One customer's eyes rolled back in his head when he swallowed the moist, buttery biscuit that was part of a batch Hutch just released from the oven.

Hutch placed a cloth-covered basket of them next to his father in the serving line. "I think these are going over well."

"So far," his father appraised. "But we've got some tough customers up ahead." He bent over the stack of plates to get a fresh one as Old Man Beauford approached. He was one of Last Stand's saltiest locals.

And he always ordered the same entrée with a double side of potato salad and a sweet tea. Nothing else.

Until today.

Hutch's father slyly unfolded the fabric from the basket and slipped a biscuit onto the side of Old Man Beauford's plate.

He huffed. "What's that?"

"A butter biscuit. It's on the house today."

The old man accepted the plate with one hand while he picked up the biscuit with the other. He sniffed it.

Frowned.

But he took a bite.

Then his face did the talking. It wasn't a smile. No, Old Man Beauford didn't smile. But the twitch of his lips meant approval.

Once he stepped away, Hutch's father said, "If you can get Old Man Beauford to have a reaction like that to something new around here, then you might just have a winner on your hands."

Hutch agreed.

Biscuits were cheap, so they made good financial sense. But they were also a comfort food, something few people made from scratch in their own homes anymore. With the propensity for convenience and the proliferation of heat-and-eat varieties in the store, giving someone a fresh, made-from-scratch biscuit either opened up a whole new taste bud experience or simply reawakened a former food love.

Hutch also couldn't deny the success of Cole's choice. The warm corn casserole had an inviting aroma, and it made a pleasing visual impression on plates as well.

While Hutch still held on to his position that sometimes compromises resulted in both parties losing, this particular situation showed a net gain. For him. For Cole. But, more importantly, for customers who would continue to sustain their family business.

These changes alone weren't going to offer a total sales figure turnaround, but they were at least the start toward more inclusive thinking and more confidence in trying new things.

Hutch told Cole as they neared the end of the workday, "I really think we're on to something. Good job with your choice."

"You too." Cole's sincerity shone, and his words smoothed some of the stress they had been under with deciding on menu changes.

"Working together actually—"

"Works?" Cole smirked.

"Yeah." Hutch razzed his younger brother by weaving close to him, to which Cole immediately responded with playful, wrestling-fast footwork. Hutch balled his fingers into a fist and was able to get one swift rub against the top of Cole's hair.

"Hey." He swatted his hand, ducking away. As teenagers, they often brawled, taunted, and tussled. They were boys with high levels of testosterone. "You're going to mess up my style."

"Style?" Hutch guffawed. "What style? You need a haircut."

"I'll have you know," Cole began, shaking his forehead to spread the slightly longer strands of his hair that Hutch had pushed to the side, "that this hair got a compliment over the weekend."

"Oh?" Hutch's interest was piqued because there was a twinkle in his brother's eye that suggested flattery. But Hutch wasn't going to make it easy for him to share. "Who told you lies about your looks?"

"Very funny," Cole deadpanned. "Actually, a woman had something to say."

Hutch and Cole saw women all day long. Off-the-market married ones. Middle-aged ones. Elderly ones that smelled like Avon and cookies. "That means nothing."

"It came from Quinn."

"As in, the librarian?" She wasn't married. Or middle-aged. Or elderly.

"How many Quinns do you know?"

"Only one." It wasn't a popular first name in Last Stand. "So?"

"So?" If Cole had more to say, he was now being mum.

Hutch prompted for details. "What did she say?"

"Wouldn't you like to know?" Cole turned on his heel and shut down the conversation just as fast as it began.

Cole liked attention. He was fed by it. Flattery nursed him to his very core.

But, if Hutch were honest with himself, he wasn't much different. He liked attention too, liked it very much. Though he didn't care for attention for the sake of attention. He liked when it meant something, when it came as a result of actions that mattered and from a person who did too.

And when he thought through it all, Valerie Perry washed right back in to his memory.

Why couldn't navigating the waters of female relationships ever be easy?

If Hutch didn't do something to more permanently scrub these thoughts, he was going to have a hard time getting anything done this week. A guy needed to be able to move on because he might just be in for more trouble down the road if he didn't.

Chapter Twenty

PENNY BRISTO WORKED magic.

There had been two showings on Sunday and three more scheduled for the next day. So when Penny Bristo's car pulled into the driveway at six o'clock on Monday after all the buyers had been ushered through the bungalow, Valerie crossed her fingers.

"Hi, Penny." She greeted her at the door.

The real estate agent strode into the living room like a show pony. "I have news." She could barely contain an overly wide smile.

And seeing her face made Valerie want to smile. Still, she approached with caution. "Good news?"

"Great news." Penny pulled a legal-sized envelope from her purse and held it between them.

"What's that?"

"Something you'll need to read carefully."

"Oh?" Valerie brought one hand to her chest as she accepted the envelope with the other. "I think I need to sit down."

"You should." Penny lowered herself primly onto the settee cushion next to her. "Now I'm no wizard," she began as Valerie slid her finger beneath the flap and pulled out a slim stack of papers. "But I can cast a few spells over my clients."

"I'm not in need of sorcery. Just a buyer."

"I've got one."

The words rang clear as a bell, a tune Valerie longed to hear. "You do?"

The smile that Penny was trying to hide earlier burst forth. "Yes, honey. I have brought you a buyer." She pointed her manicured fingernail in Valerie's direction. "Because I work for you."

Penny didn't need to sell herself to Valerie.

She just needed to sell.

And it sounded like she had. "An offer." Valerie whispered the words.

Penny angled her chin high in the air. "The second couple that saw the place today fell in love." She emphasized the words again. "In *love*."

Valerie nodded along.

"And they are willing to pay a price to own what they love."

Valerie could hardly believe her luck. Even though she had wanted this process to happen quickly, she privately expected it to take much longer.

"You have an opportunity to sell this house," she said simply. "So let me tell you about it." She reached for the papers in Valerie's now slackened hand. Penny fanned the pristine legal paperwork on the coffee table Valerie was now bracing her feet against as a way to stay upright. She was glad she'd decided to sit; if she hadn't, she might have collapsed to the floor from sheer surprise. "You'll be very pleased with the terms of this contract."

Valerie's eyes tried to dart as fast as Penny's fingers moved.

"It's an all-cash offer." The good news continued with a bang.

Valerie didn't need to know much in terms of the real estate business to know that was a good thing. "That's fantastic!"

"We priced it right."

I'll say.

"Fair pricing always makes my job easier." Penny leaned across to her purse and procured a ballpoint pen. She pressed the top, and the sharp click sounded like a small confetti popper.

"Is it for the full asking price?"

Penny lay the pen on the table, not meeting Valerie's eyes. "Not quite."

"Oh?"

Penny slid the papers closer to Valerie and stayed silent as she pointed to the number. It was a six-digit figure, which was more money than Valerie had ever had in a bank account or in any other version of accounts in her name.

Ever.

She stared at the number, which represented big money to her. Even minus Penny's 6 percent commission, Valerie would still walk away with a sizable amount of cash that she could put away or invest or use for a permanent home of her own someday.

So many possibilities . . .

Valerie continued to stare, and just as she readied to ask more questions about the terms, she saw something in the digits that made her pause.

And every emotion changed for her.

So did the questions she thought she would have for Penny.

She couldn't get her lips to form any of them because instead Valerie was busy chewing on a tough question that she had never bothered to ask herself before this very moment.

What was her grandmother's legacy worth to her? Her home, her sense of place, the location she loved?

Was it worth the number Valerie saw on the contract?

Or could the answer not be found behind a dollar sign?

VALERIE NEEDED TO call her parents. Penny had left the paperwork with Valerie at her request. She simply needed time to process, and she wanted to read through the contract for herself.

And now that she was actually on the cusp of doing it, hesitation pulled at her like never before.

Whether that was from the enormity of the task or her conflicting emotions, Valerie wasn't sure. What she was certain of was that she needed to feel secure in signing the document and accepting the offer, but she couldn't bring herself to do it in Penny's presence.

Valerie had promised an answer within forty-eight hours.

She sat in the center of the small settee in the living room she had transformed in order to do just that. To think. To reflect. To find confidence.

She placed the documents in her lap, their proximity her only company in the otherwise vacated space. Sure, the décor sang of its shabby chicness, but aside from things around her, she was alone.

And sometimes being alone was the best way to find what a person was looking for.

To that end, she closed her eyes and willed herself to think of the woman who was responsible for this situation.

Val Perry.

When Valerie thought of her grandmother, it was hard for her to settle on a singular image. She had her experiences along with a few photos, but there was a generational distance that she never quite understood until now. Was she loved by her grandmother? Of course. But did she know her? Not really.

Her grandmother was a widow the last two and a half decades of her life, her husband dying the year before Valerie was born. To Valerie, her grandmother's widowhood was a badge she wore as long as she had known her.

But she hadn't thought about her grandmother's love aside from roses, her home, and her community. No doubt she experienced romantic love and lived a full life of that, even though her identity was foreign to Valerie in that regard.

She squeezed her eyes, willing herself to think of it, and as she did, she juxtaposed conjured ideas with recent experiences. But they weren't of her grandmother.

In the stillness of the space and in the folds of her sweetest memories, she thought of someone else entirely.

She thought of Hutch.

Bubba Hutchinson had shown Valerie love in the tender things he did. His concern and his desire to make things right were evident from the first morning she met him. Their inaugural meeting wasn't conventional, but it sure was memorable. A smile played on her lips at the way he swung into her life, announcing himself with a bang of a tree trunk against her driveway.

What would her grandmother have said about a boy who made an entrance into her granddaughter's life in that way?

Valerie would never have the opportunity to ask her. But as she let calm sweep over her, she realized that was okay.

People were part of Valerie's life, and then they weren't. When natural circumstances caused that, there was no blame to assign, no faults to lay at anyone's feet.

But when she could control the circumstances, didn't she owe it to herself to do just that? For the sake of happiness— for the chance at love—shouldn't she try?

Valerie was alone in a home that was legally hers, but she was accompanied in that moment by the wizened voice of someone very special. In her mind and in her heart, she felt her grandmother speaking to her, with words that were sweet and satisfying.

Grandma Perry loved this place because it delivered experiences unlike ones she could have anywhere else. She drove her roots into the ground and made this place hers.

Quaint.

Lovely.

Safe.

It ticked all the boxes.

But Last Stand's people and surprises made it more than

just a place to hang a hat. That was what her grandmother had tried to show her during those summers Valerie spent with her. Experiences were what mattered, and when Valerie listened to the pulse of that, she had an answer that would change her future.

Now, she needed to talk to her parents about it. Though Valerie's father was states away, his voice of reason and understanding through her muddled emotions at the circumstances might help her make sense of what she was feeling.

She opened her eyes, pushed her independence aside, and grabbed her cell to dial her parents' number in Kentucky.

Her father answered her call with a cheery, "Hi, honey. How's it going?"

Valerie couldn't stop the cathartic torrent that burst forth in tears full of feeling that had no name.

"Honey? What's wrong?"

Nothing. Everything.

Her father's voice held the careful, kind tone it always did. "Valerie?" Regardless of how often they talked, he was always there for her. That level of support must have been taught.

By her. Grandma Perry.

Valerie inhaled a sob, finding her voice enough to say, "I don't want to sell the house."

THE LUNCHTIME SUCCESS of the new menu items lit a fire under Hutch, and it would stay lit until the *Modern Texas* editor came.

Whenever he came.

If he came.

The food guru's final words on the phone to Hutch during their conversation had been, "I'll try to get by there next week." Hutch was hanging his hopes on those words, even though they were short of a concrete promise. Still, a loose commitment was better than nothing.

Hutch had planted the seed, and he hoped that cultivating it through positive thinking would work.

He said he would try.

So that means he's going to do it.

The editor will *come.*

Versions of mental affirmation still flowed line by line through his head, even when he thought the workday was done on Tuesday.

But when it rained in the barbeque world, it poured. Just as the time was nearing to close the market's doors for the day, the editor arrived.

He asked for Hutch by name.

"I'm Hutch." He stuck out his hand, hoping it wasn't slick with stress sweat. He had seen the guy's photo online, so he had a sense of him before they stood face-to-face.

"Mister Barbeque," the editor returned, reciprocating a firm handshake. Whether he was referring to himself or assigning Hutch a nickname, he wasn't sure. Either way was fine by him.

"It's a pleasure to meet you." Hutch stood star struck.

"Not every place is open early in the week like this." The editor finished the handshake and looked around the interior as they spoke. "Big places in the city, for sure. But out in places like here—"

"We're open today," Hutch assured him. "Come in." He tried his best to make him feel welcome, giving him wide physical space while ushering him further to have a seat.

"Homey." His judgment in a one-word appraisal was hard to read.

Hutch wanted to focus on what they did best. "Our barbeque may remind you of home. It's comfort food around here. And we've got a pretty full slate of it."

"Even now?" The editor raised a skeptical eyebrow as he checked his watch.

"We have some big orders later." A little white lie seemed acceptable, given the circumstance. Besides, for all Hutch knew, they might. "But we've got all the classics." He rattled off their offerings, then pointed to the menu board. "And sides." He was shy about committing to the new dishes but decided to mention the biscuits and corn casserole in the litany of others since they had gone over well the last two days. "They're experimental but, um . . ." He cleared his throat. "We like to give our customers something fresh here. You know, local ingredients."

"So you have hot sides and cold sides?" He seemed to be making a mental note.

"Yes, sir." Every word was a forced commitment. Hutch felt pricked by responsibility to get this right without blowing the chance. Where was Cole? Shouldn't he introduce him as the new family partner? Surely youth would set the place apart in the editor's mind. Pressure closed in around Hutch, and how sweat wasn't pouring from his forehead and drenching the poor guy was beyond him.

"I'll eat anything. I may not like everything I eat," he warned, "but I'll eat it."

Great. Hutch forced an uncomfortable chuckle. He reached his hand to the back of his neck, landing on the instant knot of tension that formed. "I'll bring you a sampler platter."

"Sounds good." The man reached into his jacket pocket and brought out a small notebook. Very journalistic. But very old-school journalistic.

Whatever gets the job done.

Hutch lowered his hand and remembered to ask before he disappeared into the kitchen. "Can I get you a drink?"

"A glass of the sweetest tea you've got."

That was language Hutch understood. "Coming right up."

The Hut wasn't set up for full service, but Hutch didn't mind waiting on this special customer. This was make-or-break time. He'd asked for this. And he wasn't about to let the opportunity to help secure the future of The Hut through positive statewide press slip through his fingers.

As Hutch turned, he nearly ramrodded into Cole. "There you are." He hissed under his breath. He reached for his forearm and turned back to the editor. "Allow me to introduce my brother, Cole. We're partners in this venture."

"Co-owners?" The man kept his notepad at the ready.

Hutch released his grip, swung his arm about the shoulders of his brother, and summoned his happiest sibling look. "Yes. We're taking the place over from our parents." He spoke with every swell of pride he felt. "We're third generation here."

"That's impressive." The man scribbled a note. "Longevity is important. It creates institutions." He was speaking their language. "Memorable locations. And experiences."

"That's what we're about here."

The editor narrowed his eyes. "You know," he spoke thoughtfully. "Some people read us online, but lots still buy our magazine based on the cover." He looked from Cole to Hutch and back again. "And a couple of barbeque brothers like you would make a mighty impressive image splashed across it."

Cover models?

Hutch didn't know he had a streak of vanity until his ego was stroked with that idea. He was hoping for some interior coverage, but free advertising on the cover of the state's most prominent magazine sounded good too.

Hutch squeezed Cole's shoulder, his enthusiasm needing an outlet. He didn't want to get ahead of himself, but this was already more promising than he could have imagined. "Let me get that tea for you. Cole, why don't you tell the man about our pits? Maybe even take a little tour later."

"Sure." Cole slid into the type of conversation that was as natural to him as breathing. Pitmastering was his wheelhouse.

And, if everything went smoothly for the rest of the editor's visit, the rest of the state might just get a glimpse into that too.

Chapter Twenty-One

F RONT-YARD SPACE WAS something Valerie never had and never wanted. But she adored watering what survived of her grandmother's antique roses. She enjoyed tending to the new plants Hutch placed into the ground. And she liked filling the window boxes built by Carlos with soil, flowers, and mulch.

After spending a week and a half in the bungalow, surrounded by the community her grandmother adored, Valerie experienced an ownership over her inheritance that was more than surface level. There was pride in the place and love for what it represented that tugged at her.

She prized the front yard, and the same was now true of the backyard. She especially enjoyed it filled with people like it had been on Saturday night. The crisp outdoor air, the twinkling stars overhead, the chatter of conversation amid lapping flames from the fire pit. It had all been so idyllic.

And the little things added up. Small pleasures made a big difference in her attitude and her feeling of contentment, like the delicious s'mores grilled on the fire pit. That was something she couldn't do in her no patio, no outdoor space apartment. But with the fire pit at the bungalow, she would use it all the time. Valerie pictured herself grilling fresh vegetables, kabobs, portobello mushroom burgers. A vegetarian could do a lot with fire.

Valerie smiled to herself at not just recent memories of the bungalow but future ones as well. She had never experienced such a strong yearning for one place to serve permanently as her home.

Maybe she was idealizing, but what if . . .

Valerie dialed her office's main phone number. "I need to speak with someone in HR." There was no way she could keep two homes. And she wasn't about to quit her job. She needed the income, and she loved the work too much. But just maybe . . .

If there was a way to make this work, she would fight for it.

Because if her time in Last Stand had taught her anything, it was that places carried special meaning. This bungalow did that for Grandma Perry. And perhaps all along, Grandma Perry knew that it could do the same for Valerie.

She spent a tense hour on the phone. The Human Resources staff member admitted that the company was open to workplace solutions. She explained a new initiative for telecommuting the company was just beginning to explore.

"We don't have the details worked out yet. But you might be a good first case, based on your positive work history and track record of effective digital reporting."

Valerie's supervisor was looped into the call, and she expressed support for the initiative. "You know we value your skills as a buyer."

Considering all the produce and fruit possibilities, the Texas Hill Country was ripe for the picking. "My skills are going to be so much more valuable on the ground where the food is grown." She gave her final push as she summoned the same confidence she used in her initial interview with the buying team. "We'll be able to source better quality and develop more effective routes for delivery if I telecommute."

"You'll still have to come into the office at certain times throughout the year," her supervisor said.

"Of course." Occasional trips to San Antonio would help her keep her feet wet in the city.

"I'll have to draw up a contract, and there will be details to hammer out." Human Resources would help with that.

"Naturally."

"Then let's try telecommuting."

Only when Valerie was assured she had full support and a plan for moving forward on the paperwork did she thank her supervisor and the Human Resources staff member, click off the call, and exhale a tumbleweed-sized crush of tension that had built in her chest during the conversation.

She set the phone on the counter. She was alone in the bungalow, but she didn't feel lonely. Valerie sensed her grandmother's arms wrapping her in a congratulatory hug. She embraced the vibes. "I bet you never thought this place would be getting Wi-Fi," she joked.

Now there was one other tough call to make. And doing so was going to be as problematic as a skunk at a garden party.

And probably stink as badly too.

Valerie picked up the phone one final time to dial Blue-bonnet Realty.

"What?" Penny's voice shrieked so loudly that Valerie

219

had to hold the phone from her ear.

She was glad this conversation wasn't taking place face-to-face. She could imagine the way Penny's face was contorting at the turn of events. Not that she took any pleasure in the fact. "I've made an alternative decision."

Penny tried to assuage Valerie. "You must have cold feet. That's all."

This wasn't some trip to the altar. "No, I've rethought my priorities."

"Money should be your priority."

It had been. Even Valerie could admit that. But money only did so much.

She had a responsibility to her grandmother's legacy, but she also was responsible for her own future. She didn't have all the details figured out, but she knew one piece of the puzzle. "I'm keeping the house. For now."

"You're making a mistake."

Of course Penny would say that. And maybe Valerie was. But it was her mistake to make. What she knew at this very moment was that selling the house didn't feel right. And she couldn't, in good conscious, enter into such a big decision without feeling completely confident in her steps.

"Penny, you have done great work, and I appreciate you. Truly," Valerie added healing words that she hoped would smooth over any sour feelings. "You didn't sell this house, but you sold me. You sold me on the charm of this bungalow, the beauty of this neighborhood, and the possibilities of this town."

"Is there anything I can do to change your mind about actually selling?"

"No." Valerie was firm in her choice. "I want to take the house off the market."

"Temporarily?" She could hear the longing in Penny's voice.

"For the foreseeable future," she corrected Penny. "I'm just not ready to let it go."

"Fair." Penny might have been biting back more. Surely she had things to say. Yet she stayed professional. "When you are, call me."

Valerie could give her that. "I will." She thanked Penny again, and as she clicked off the call, a wave of satisfaction settled into her for a decision that felt right.

With the bungalow, Valerie wasn't just getting the four walls and a roof. She was getting comfort. And in Last Stand, she was getting friends like Quinn. Neighbors of all variety like Nod, whose sweet face she still couldn't resist.

But most importantly, if he'd have her, she might even get a future with Bubba Hutchinson, the most unlikely of men for her on paper but who, in reality, checked off all the boxes for Valerie.

Except for his love of meat.

She smiled to herself at the very thought because, if that was his only liability, she could learn to live with that.

But there was a bigger question to ask, and she needed to know. Could Hutch live with the reality of who she was? Did they have a future? Or had she completely blown the opportunity by not realizing what she wanted until she had already pushed him away?

"YOU BOYS HAVE really impressed me." Wanda Hutchinson's eyes shone with the satisfaction of a mother who had raised her children well.

"I'll second that." Todd sidled up next to her wearing a similar expression.

Hutch and Cole stood before them, two generations yoked together by their shared love of the family business.

It had been a long Thursday, and business had been good.

Real good.

They'd find out just how good in a few moments when their mother ran the report from the cash register. But, even without hard and fast numbers, they all knew.

Customer traffic seemed to be spurred by word of the *Modern Texas* editor being in town. Gossip in Last Stand spread faster than pink eye. And this was good gossip. After all, it wasn't every day that the town received surprise publicity visits. Word traveled fast about the magazine's interest in The Hut.

The timing was perfect, too, because churning in the rumor mill was also talk about the new side dishes available. Never had biscuits and corn casserole dominated conversations.

The Hut's barbeque was still king, though it was nice to have royalty alongside it with their additional menu offerings.

Locals who had been long dormant along with fair weather customers came in droves after the editor left. The excitement was palpable, and the interest was so intense it could practically be forked with barbeque prongs. Everyone wanted to get a taste of what The Hut had.

Hutch kept his own enthusiasm tempered. "We still don't know what he's going to write."

"That guy was hard to read," Cole apprised.

"Regardless," his father insisted, "getting him here was a good call."

"And I can't imagine he'll have anything negative to say." That was Wanda's optimism talking. Still, Hutch wanted to believe his mother. They all did.

"He didn't seem to lean in that direction." Though Hutch really had no measure for that. Still, the extra foot traffic was a welcome boost. "Think about this. If just hearing about the guy got this many people through the doors, what would an actual feature do?"

"Or a cover photo?" Wanda winked.

Hutch had, naturally, shared that bit with his mom. It was hard to keep such a major possibility to himself.

"Let's just keep doing what we're doing." Cole was right. Although the food editor's visit had gone smoothly, there wasn't much to go on regarding next steps. Hutch and Cole saw him take notes, but he didn't make further small talk after his food arrived. They weren't sure whether he liked everything they offered him because his lips stayed mum.

But he did finish every bite of food they gave him. For Hutch, he was hanging his hopes on that very fact. After all, would someone who disliked the food have cleared his plate?

"We hadn't seen such a crowd in a long time." His dad would know.

And the crowd came early.

Folks started lining up to get brisket when it first became

available at ten thirty a.m. Ribs were the next to go, followed by sellouts of every other piece of meat on the pits.

"Today was a good sales day." Wanda nodded before turning to the cash register to confirm her assessment with actual numbers.

"Let me know the grand total," Hutch called to her.

"Me too," Cole added.

Their father turned toward the kitchen while Cole did the same at the pits. Hutch strode toward the front entrance, readying his hand to turn the *open* sign to *closed* just as a final customer approached.

He was ready to say the requisite "I'm sorry we're all sold out of barbeque" line, but as he looked toward the face opposite the glass, he didn't need those words.

Not for a vegetarian.

"Valerie." Her name sprang to his lips in a whisper. He swung open the door, and the situation was oddly reminiscent of their first meeting.

At an entrance.

On personal property.

Caught by surprise.

But this wasn't the bungalow and theirs wasn't a first meeting.

Yet, as Hutch held open the door, it had the force of one.

"Hello, Bubba." Valerie held on to the use of that name, and Hutch wasn't rattled by it. He still wasn't sure why.

He tipped his head in greeting. "Would you like to come in?" He wouldn't make the invitation for anyone, but his mind had just shifted from wanting to close up the entrance to wanting to make it a revolving door for this woman.

Because even before her arm grazed against his in passing, Hutch's skin prickled with an electric jolt of longing. Valerie's hair trailed atop her shoulder, bouncing in time with her steps. A loose strand hung in front of her ear, and Hutch had to stop himself from reaching toward her to tuck it gently back into place.

Valerie stepped inside and paused a few feet in front of him. He couldn't help sneaking a peek of admiration at her figure. She turned just as Hutch snapped his head to attention. She looked like she wanted to speak, but no words formed.

"If you came here looking for lunch, I'm sorry to have to tell you—"

"I'm not here for lunch," she cut in.

Her fast rate of speech caught him off guard. "Oh?"

She reached up to the loose strand of hair and tucked it behind her ear exactly as Hutch would have done before looking him straight in the eye. "I'm here for something else."

Hutch's palms started sweating, and his heart rallied into a quickened beat. "And what might that be?"

"I'm here," she began again, her words meaningful and her tone sincere, "to let you know I'm not selling the bungalow."

Hutch had expected more than a line about a house. Maybe that was just his wishful thinking. He tried to will his heartbeat to slow. "So you're a homeowner then. Congratulations," he added with little fanfare.

"I was hoping for a bit more than that."

"More than what?"

Valerie held his gaze, drawing them together with just a look that made him question more than what he asked.

But when Valerie didn't answer, Hutch asked again in a different way.

"What are you wanting, Valerie? Why are you here?"

Hutch had been blown away by surprises before. But nothing prepared him for the shock of Valerie Perry's answer.

"I want to make a life in Last Stand. And I'm here," Valerie drew a deep breath, "because I want to know if you'll be a part of it too."

❧

"DOES THIS POST oak look healthy to you?" Valerie shielded her eyes from the glare of the sun, looking into the canopy that covered the bungalow's backyard.

"It's dead."

"Seriously?" Valerie narrowed her gaze, trying to see what Hutch was seeing.

But his laughter broke her concentration. "You are too easy."

Burned.

Again.

Hutch had a sense of humor Valerie was still getting used to, but, based on the time they'd spent together the past few weeks, she had been adjusting.

She also hadn't lost her sass. "And you"—she brought her hand down—"should be ashamed of yourself for thinking of my trees as your next source of barbeque pit fuel."

"Guilty." He held up his hands in mock arrest. "My mind's always on barbeque."

"When it's not on other things . . ." Valerie trailed suggestively.

"I like the way you think." Hutch reached to her waist, pulling her in close. "And I like the way you kiss." He bent into her, their lips flirting with a slight tease before cementing shared attraction in a kiss they both savored.

She nipped at his lower lip before pulling back, soliciting a sexy smirk from Hutch. His face radiated a warmth that Valerie felt. She leaned back, resting into the embrace of his arms. She wanted to stay in this hold forever.

And now that she was making a life in Last Stand, she could.

The End

The Hut's Barbeque Sauce

This all-purpose sauce can be used on ribs and chicken or to accompany smoked sausage or brisket. Experiment with more or less of the spices to fit your preferred taste.

2 T. Worcestershire sauce
2 T. lemon juice
1 tsp. paprika
1 tsp. salt
1 tsp. black pepper
¾ cup ketchup
¾ cup water
½ cup finely chopped onion

Mix all ingredients. Cook over low heat. Keep cooking low and slow until your desired consistency.

Beef Brisket

This isn't quite as good as what The Hut makes using post oak wood, but it's still a delicious version to serve at home.

1 medium-sized brisket, market trimmed

3 T. Worcestershire sauce

3 T. soy sauce

1 T. liquid smoke

½ t. seasoned salt

½ t. onion salt

½ t. garlic salt

½ t. black pepper

Put brisket on large piece of foil. Mix all other ingredients together. Pour over the brisket. Wrap tightly. Refrigerate for 24 hours. Then, bake at 250 degrees for approximately 5 hours. Slice and serve with The Hut's barbeque sauce on the side.

Tailgate Tomato and Cucumber Salad

This is perfect for a picnic or for any gathering where you need to make a dish ahead of time. Use the freshest vegetables for the best taste.

4 garden grown cucumbers, sliced
3 garden grown tomatoes, wedged
1 sweet Vidalia onion, sliced
1 c. water
¼ c. oil
¼ c. sugar
½ c. vinegar
1 tsp. salt
¼ tsp. black pepper

Mix all ingredients. Chill until ready to eat. Use a slotted spoon to serve.

Bubba Hutchinson's Country Biscuits

These biscuits are a simple addition to any meal. Make sure to keep extra butter on hand for brushing across the top of the biscuits before serving. These can be eaten plain or with jam.

2 c. flour

1 T. sugar

1 T. baking powder

¾ cup milk

6 T. butter, grated (placing a stick of butter in the freezer for 20 minutes makes it easy to grate)

Mix all ingredients. Batter will be lumpy. Shape, form, or press into a biscuit cutter to make 6-8 biscuits. Place on ungreased baking sheet. Bake at 450 degrees for 10-12 minutes. Brush with butter while still warm.

If you enjoyed this book, please leave a review at your favorite online retailer! Even if it's just a sentence or two it makes all the difference.

Thanks for reading *On the Market* by Audrey Wick!

Discover your next romance at TulePublishing.com.

TULE
PUBLISHING

If you enjoyed *On the Market,* you'll love the next book in….

The Texas BBQ Brothers series

Book 1: *On the Market*

Book 2: *Off the Market*

Available now at your favorite online retailer!

About the Author

Audrey Wick is a full-time English professor at Blinn College in Texas. Her writing has appeared in college textbooks published by Cengage Learning and W. W. Norton as well as in *The Houston Chronicle, The Chicago Tribune, The Orlando Sentinel,* and various literary journals. Audrey believes the secret to happiness includes lifelong learning and good stories. But travel and coffee help. She has journeyed to over twenty countries—and sipped coffee at every one. Connect with her at audreywick.com and @WickWrites.

Thank you for reading

On the Market

If you enjoyed this book, you can find more from all our great authors at TulePublishing.com, or from your favorite online retailer.

TULE
PUBLISHING